The Doctor's Promise

The Doctor's Promise

Elizabeth Seifert

Thorndike Press • Chivers Press
Thorndike, Maine USA Bath, England

This Large Print edition is published by Thorndike Press, USA
and by Chivers Press, England.

Published in 2000 in the U.S. by arrangement with
Spectrum Literary Agency

Published in 2000 in the U.K. by arrangement with
Ralph Vicinanza Ltd

U.S. Hardcover 0-7862-2491-6 (Romance Series Edition)
U.K. Hardcover 0-7540-4137-9 (Chivers Large Print)

The text of this Large Print edition is unabridged.
Other aspects of the book may vary from the original edition.

Set in 16 pt. Plantin by Minnie B. Raven.

Printed in the United States on permanent paper.

British Library Cataloguing-in-Publication Data available

Library of Congress Cataloging-in-Publication Data

Seifert, Elizabeth, 1897–
The doctor's promise / by Elizabeth Seifert.
p. cm.
ISBN 0-7862-2491-6 (lg. print : hc : alk. paper)
1. Physicians — Middle West — Family relationships — Fiction. 2. Middle West — Fiction. 3. Large type books.
I. Title.
PS3537.E352 D66 2000
813′.52—dc21 00-021253

The Doctor's Promise

Chapter 1

Dick shifted unhappily in his chair. "I have to take off forty pounds, or pass a motion for bigger chairs," he told himself. A three-day meeting. For him? A general practitioner with patients overflowing his office, forty others scattered in the three hospitals that recorded Dr. Richard Foster as on their staffs. General, Children's, and Research. And he'd had words with each institution about their bulletin board's listings. He was *not* an internist. He was a G.P., and proud to be the last of a dying race.

"Are you listening?" asked the man at his side. Kenneth Harrington, his assistant, his friend, and on the way to be, maybe, a better doctor than was Dick. A very nice guy, Kenneth, friendly, unflappable.

Dick envied him.

Should he listen? He guessed so. If ever they were to have a medical school in this city, the doctors who would work with it should know what was going on, or about to go on. He looked down at the program which he had rolled into a pencil-thin tube.

He looked up at the speaker behind the desk. Podium? He unrolled the tube of slick paper. Docents? That was the title of his lecture which was slated to last all morning.

"What's a docent?" he whispered to Kenneth.

"Listen and you'll find out."

"Where's Jan?"

"Back in the corner, behind the piano. Wives were not asked to come."

"Anybody brave enough to tell her so?"

"Shut up and listen."

So Dick shut up, he unbuttoned his jacket and slumped down in the uncomfortable chair. The lecturer was holding the audience. He had a good voice and spoke his words precisely. But he addressed the assembled surgeons and physicians as he probably addressed his classes of pre-med students. Considering them all to be idiots, needing to have every fact explained. All right. So what were docents?

They were pre-medical students who were to work with some of the assembled doctors in an experiment. Dick closed his mind. He did not have time for experiments. Kenneth jogged his arm.

"The new approach to training doctors is not radical," the speaker declared. "We are hoping to pick up and use trends which have been around medical education for some time. Our students will eventually be taking the national board exams like any medical school graduates, and our reputation for teaching them may rest on the shoulders of you doctors who are interested in the establishment of a medical school in this city. We, at present, do not have that medical school, we do not have the traditional faculty and curriculum to present to our pre-medical students. So we must build a program. This need is what I shall talk about. It is called the docent program. About two years of standard pre-medical training in the arts as well as some of the scientific things he must know — in chemistry, biology, and so on — the student will be assigned to a teacher, a docent. The docent becomes the student's director, teacher, and counselor until he graduates, and we hope is ready for full-time assignment to a medical school. The two years he has with us well may shorten that four-year course to three, and, in time, to two. During his pre-medical years he still will have some studies in the arts, but he will also have a lot of studies in the medical field. He will be trained by doctors successfully practicing what he will need to know. The docent is a doctor of a particular sort. He is a scholar and a practicing physician."

"And busy," said Dick Foster in a clearly heard comment.

"And busy," agreed the lecturer enthusiastically.

"You'd better keep still," Kenneth warned his partner.

"Now you tell me."

"Listen," said Kenneth.

". . . busy doctor willing to cut into his office practice in order to introduce these students to patients, starting with the first day of class, and then he guides the students in the concepts and needs that relate to the patients' needs."

He paused, looking around the room. "Now this is the essential definition of the program I plan to discuss."

There was a spate of questions, comments. Who had thought this up? Was the A.M.A. behind it? All sorts of things. Dick stood up to stretch his legs and ease his back. "I am not used to sitting down," he explained. He was a big man, but not overweight in any sense. His skin was clear, his very blue eyes the best feature after his smile, which was a fine, open smile that crinkled his eyes and wreathed his lips. His voice was warm and sincere.

He looked across the room. "Where did

Jan go?" he asked Kenneth.

"Maybe she went down the hall. Why did she come?"

"She was not invited."

"But she came anyway."

"As you can plainly see. I told her the weather would be terrible."

"So the sun shines and the breeze is fresh."

"Don't forget the autumn leaves. I told her none of the other wives ever attended this sort of thing."

"And she came to find out why."

"She came because I told her not to. D'you think we'll get that medical school?"

"Not on the docent project alone."

"There's a lot of interest in having the school. And surely we have teaching hospitals enough."

"But do we have money enough?"

"I think the money can be found. We doctors will get nicked for a share, and we would find it a valuable asset to have a medical school with our own interns and residents."

"I'll pledge ten cents," said Dick, sitting down again. "Would you care to go out and get me a hot dog?" he asked Kenneth.

"Where do they sell hot dogs? It's fried chicken, or pizzas, or coney dogs, or tacos. And we'd better shut up; our friend wants to talk again."

"With charts, yet."

The speaker did have charts. Marked with crosses and circles and dotted lines. They didn't look like medical students to him, said a voice from across the room. Janice Foster returned to her chair. She was a small, compact woman, with a smoothly browned skin. Her black hair was cut short, and had a way of straggling across her forehead. Purposely? Dick asked himself. He was often tempted to put those dark strands back from her face. She never wore makeup, and had small skill with clothes. But she was firm in the ideas she had, persistent in the purposes she defined for herself. Dick wished she had stayed at home that weekend. Kenneth was sure that Dick had not asked his wife to attend this meeting.

As if he read his companion's thoughts, Dick said softly, musingly, "Jan says I am a very bad husband."

"Are you?"

"I suppose I am. Do you want me to quote Crowninshield to you?"

"Not again," laughed his partner.

But Dick whispered the words. *Married men make very bad husbands.*

He'd quote it to people — friends, associates, even patients — who asked how he had happened to marry Jan. It was the only answer he had. It was hard for him to remember the grinding fatigue, the essential loneliness of internship.

So even Dick wondered how he and Jan had ever got together in the first place. Often, he wondered. Jan could be getting nothing from their marriage. They had a pleasant home, no children, and their interests were poles apart. It was typical that Jan had insisted on coming to this meeting; Dick hoped devoutly that she would take no part in it. He never, willingly, let her share his professional activities.

The speaker — leader — rapped for order. He was ready to speak more specifically, he said.

"She thought you were going to bring Leslie," murmured Kenneth.

So Dick thought about Leslie while he watched the leader explain his charts, using an old-fashioned wooden pointer with a rubber tip. Where had he ever found that thing?

Leslie. Yes! Better to think about than Jan. Leslie Jackson was Dick's medical secretary, and invaluable in his office. Out of it, as well, because she gave him what Jan did not. Leslie admired Dr. Foster, she shielded him, she helped him, and when occasion permitted, she loved him. She was a smiling, scrubbed-clean-looking girl with a nice figure, a pleasant voice, and thick, pretty blond hair. She wore suits and sweater blouses, and looked well in them. Dick liked her, and found comfort in her. He wished she had come to this meeting with him, instead of Jan. He looked across the room. Yes. His wife was back, seated in a far corner, listening intently, as he had better do.

Someone had asked a question, and the pointer tapped the chart. They were planning to start with three docents, each with twelve students. Eventually they hoped to have thirty-two docents in the area.

Did they have that many doctors to be teachers? That many students who — ?

"No, we cannot require participation, but a student who has taken the program before he enters medical school is months ahead of the ones who don't."

"How much of the doctor's time will it take?" Dick asked.

"That of course depends on the docent and the student. Our schedule calls for the medical student to spend twelve weeks of each year making patient rounds with the doctor-docent. During the rest of that year he will regularly see patients on an office or home basis, under supervision, of course."

Somebody made a wisecrack about finding a docent who saw his own patients in the home.

"I do," said Dick Foster.

So did Kenneth Harrington.

This stirred up a discussion, even an argument, certainly delay.

Someone said that if one docent showed his students home circumstances, all should be required.

"I think the home calls should be omitted; they are unrealistic."

Dick and Kenny had their heads together while Dick scribbled on the margin of the program. He stood up and asked for the floor. He pointed out that the planners of this program were the unrealistic ones. Had they figured how many hours would be required for a doctor to give each of twelve students twelve week and for a hundred and thirty-two . . . ?

"Go over your arithmetic, sir," he advised.

"And do what?"

"Give each of the docents six students, with six weeks each of intensive instruction, including one week in his own home. And, I suppose, monthly meetings of the docent's group, maybe all meeting occasionally. But get the figures straight, sir. Get them straight!"

So there were arguments. One doctor declared that no one was going to tell him what to do!

Kenneth Harrington groaned.

"Participation will be voluntary, Dr. Truesdell," said the lecturer coldly, "but once a doctor is a docent, I think certain rules must prevail."

"Depends," said Dr. Truesdell, an older man than most of those who had gathered. "Does this so-called student go to school?"

"Oh, yes. He keeps the same patients he acquired from his docent, and reports on them. But he will take the regular courses given and required by his college. And when he enters medical school — here in this city, we hope — he will continue to work with his docent."

"That means five years," said Dick thoughtfully.

"Yes, it does, Doctor. He can learn a lot in that time."

"He? Won't some of them . . . ?"

"There are more women declaring for medicine right along. Yes, there would be women. We have another idea which we hope will appeal to you. That is for the docent teams to visit various neighborhood health centers and other areas outside of the hospital and office. Perhaps we shall eventually decide to put the entire emphasis on the inner city."

"I don't see how the school pre-med education thing can be oriented with your program," someone said.

"I know. There may be difficulties. We won't — we don't — have traditional departments such as biochemistry and anatomy. But don't you think the student will learn a great deal on these subjects from personal contacts with the patients, and then can more easily relate his book studies to the patient?"

"You would have specialists lecture or demonstrate?"

"Be better to allow attendance to the lectures and demonstrations already being carried on for the medical school students. Even before we have our hoped-for school, busloads of eager pre-med students could go to other schools, or even attend medical society meetings right here in the city."

"That's a proper suggestion, Doctor," said the lecturer. "I am sure it would be used."

"Do you have some sort of center?" asked Dick Foster. "Since we don't at this moment have any university-owned hospital."

"There isn't a medical school either," Truesdell piped up.

The lecturer remained patient. "Until our medical school building is completed — we hope in two years — the docent program students would be based in the former nursing residence at Research Hospital."

There was a marked lack of enthusiasm. "It would serve!" Dick said angrily. "And I would suggest that these students see patients in the city-owned General Hospital. You get a broad spectrum, and less flap — though of course Research and Children's would gradually cooperate. Both do a lot of charitable work."

"Yes, they do, but your suggestion is a good one. Our program is designed to produce doctors who care about people. And to do that they must know more than the superb basic scientist, the surgeon who specializes in a certain rare heart operation, or a physician who knows and teaches all there is to know about a certain rare disease. You've all met them, you've studied under them, and you got your M.D.'s and went out into the world, ready and willing, but untrained, to treat the woman with the peptic ulcer, the diabetic, and all those with non-exotic diseases. You learned but you were not taught."

"Student doctors don't always want to learn about non-exotic diseases."

"I know they don't and our new medical

school must find room for the scientist to carry on the research desires or whatever it is he does want."

"I know we have a pretty good roster of pre-med students at the State U. here in the city. Would they be required to enter the docent program? I mean, some medical schools . . ."

"This program would be voluntary. It is hoped that the merits of the program will sell itself to the students and to the medical school." The lecturer spoke somewhat stiffly.

"Look," said Dick Foster. "We can go on talking in circles all day, and personally — You've explained the program, you've not asked for a vote of confidence, but you will. Then can we go home? We are all busy —"

"I agree with the talking in circles bit," said the leader. "And so I shall proceed to give you the conclusions reached by the committee which I represent. Remember? Your own medical society appointed them. All right! So I am authorized to name the first three docents as being the right ones to initiate our program."

There was a dead silence. All faces were turned to the man on the platform. Some were eager, some wary, a couple were stubborn. Dick Foster's was one of the stubborn ones. He knew that the city had to prepare for the new medical school, but he simply did not have the time! Besides, he had family problems. That, with a too-big practice —

But there it came. Three names. The first, "Dr. John Utley," the middle one, "Dr. Richard Foster" and — dear Lawd! the third one, "Dr. James Truesdell." This was what startled Dick, though Kenny thought —

"We've been talking about it," he told his senior.

"Not about my working with Truesdell."

"No-o. Wonder why they named him."

"He probably asked for it. He isn't in favor, and he'll try to scuttle it."

"Which you can prevent."

"I sure —" Dick began, then said in a subdued tone, "will. Look, Harrington — I can't *do* this! I'm too damned busy. I'm the last of the G.P.'s, and where will they get students who want to enter my service?"

Kenny pointed to the podium where a gavel was being rapped smartly against wood. "Dr. Foster?" asked the leader. "Do you have comments to make?"

Dick stood up and hitched at his belt. "I sure do!" he said loudly. "I don't suppose your committee had too easy a job selecting the first three goats, but I don't feel that I should be one of them. Utley's okay if he wants the position. I think we are asking a lot of Truesdell at his age —"

This set Truesdell off into a sputter of ten fuses, and there were smiles all around the room. Truesdell had begun as a G.P., but lately he was listing himself as a cancer specialist. He was not certified, though he did have a row of certificates that said he had attended a certain number of cancer clinics.

"I'm a G.P.," Dick shouted above Truesdell's voice. "I really am one. I believe in 'em, and I know we need to train more of them. The purpose of this meeting was to determine what we would need to do during the next year to ready us for the medical school. I came hoping I could lobby for a service in primary medicine. But docents? Mercy me, gentlemen, have any of you looked at my patient roster lately? Do any of you see what goes on in our waiting room? I've taken on an assistant, and I work him to death, but the cases keep coming in. How can I find time to docent even six students? Let me cite just one of my patients. I have this woman who came to me saying she had syphilis. I referred her to a gynecologist. She had already seen several, maybe some of you here in this room. Anyway, these specialists all told her she was mistaken. She did not have syphilis. Finally, for one reason or another, she reached me and my office. I had the proper tests made, told her that they were negative, but she kept coming back, she keeps coming back. She has a phobia, of course, and a nerve-injection placebo is the only thing. But how do you docent a case like that? And I get all sorts of the same stripe. I wouldn't be any good for your program, sir."

"Are you refusing, Dr. Foster?" asked the lecturer. "What you have just said confirms our opinion that you would make an excellent docent. We know you are busy. We took that fact into consideration. And we decided that a busy doctor was exactly what the docent program would need. A doctor who could teach the students what they were getting into. In short, we want at least one busy docent who will produce more busy G.P.'s."

Dick made growling sounds and started to sit down. Then he rose to his full height, which was over six feet. "There's another thing," he said. "Where do I get room for my twelve — or even six — students?"

"They won't all function at once, Doctor. And surely you can let one student at a time sit in the corner of your office, stand at your shoulder —"

"Some patients will object."

"Yes, they might. You could present the situation to them before the student himself shows up. We expect them to have been teachable as to tact, silence —"

There were some students present, and their heads bobbed up and down. "I'd pretend the patient was my grandmother," said one young man.

"Don't tell her that!" cried Dick in alarm. "No woman wants to be told that she looks and acts like a grandmother. Which brings me to another point. Why did you choose me along with two men that are older? I can tell you it makes me feel old to be bundled into a project with two fellas who are fifty or more. Truesdell is."

This set Truesdell sputtering again. Dr. Utley only shrugged and said he'd learned things with each year. Kenneth Harrington openly laughed at Dick, and the students did, too.

Ruefully, Dick rubbed his head. "See how my bald spot is coming along," he said sheepishly. His blond hair was as thick as thatch.

And in the midst of the rising laughter and comment over this argument, heads began to turn toward the corner of the room where a small, determined figure had emerged from behind the piano, and a clear, determined voice was trying to make itself heard.

"Doctor . . ." the woman said ineffectually. Then *"Doctor!"* again more clearly, more loudly. She wore a pink blouse and a dark skirt. Her black hair was cut short, and, yes, strands of it were etched across her forehead.

Dick Foster groaned softly. "I'm leaving," he told Kenneth.

Dr. Harrington caught at his arm. "Sit tight," he said firmly. "The guys here all know you."

"But Jan —"

"Sit still, I tell you. Leaving will only —"

"Yes, Mrs. Foster," the director was saying courteously. The room quieted, and Jan moved forward so that all could see her. "I have another argument," she said clearly, "against Dr. Foster's being chosen as one of your docents. I don't think my husband could possibly do it."

Dick's every muscle stiffened. Kenny still held his arm. He was sure that Dick would someday "kill" Janice, but this should not be the time or the place. "Too many witnesses," he said under his breath. There was motive, certainly.

"I think," said Mrs. Foster, walking slowly to the front of the room, "that your docent program stinks. The whole system as you've outlined it sounds like bad business to me. If a doctor is good, or at least popular, he has too many patients. If he does have the time, he probably has nothing to teach. I think you should wait until you do have your medical school and then teach the would-be doctors in the usual way. If my word has any weight, I say *no* to the docent program, and a very definite *no* to Dr. Foster's sharing in it. He is busy, he has a home, he has his health to consider. And six years! No doctor, him least of all, will hang around and do that sort of drudgery."

Dick jerked free of Kenneth's hand, stood up and walked out of the room. His face was stone white. Jan turned to watch him go, then smiled a little and shrugged. But few saw what she did, or cared. To a man, the doctors were embarrassed, and wondered what they would do under similar circumstances. Their wives — The students looked at the woman curiously, and at the other doctors.

"I think a docent is needed right now," drawled one of them, a tall, slender black man.

The whole matter was shocking. Kenneth sought out the speaker. "I have to find Dick," he explained.

"We'll break. Nothing more could be accomplished this morning." He turned to find his gavel, to rap it sharply, and rap it again.

"I think we should adjourn," he said. "We shall —"

"Who's going to win this one?" asked a voice from the back of the room.

The leader pressed his lips together. "Will the secretary please note the names of the selected docents — or do I hear a motion to the contrary? Voting members of the Medical Society only."

There was a thundering silence.

"Then," said the leader, "we shall adjourn for lunch and reconvene at one-thirty. Members and invited guests."

Which meant the students. No one spoke to Jan as they passed her. She stood smiling, pleased with what she had done.

"Who *is* going to win this war?" the speaker asked Kenneth.

"I devoutly hope Dick will."

"He didn't seem — Is there a chance he will leave?"

"I hope not. No one could take his place. And he is a busy doctor, my friend. But he does not let his wife dictate to him in professional matters."

"You know him well?"

"Yes. I know him very well."

"I was surprised to see you both here for the meetings."

"Dick arranged it. Two friends are taking his really urgent calls, and the office is closed. He is very interested in getting a good medical school here."

"We'll get one. Could it be," said the director. "It's none of my business, but I'll speak anyway. Could it be that he is training you to take his place, that he actually is leaving?"

"He's training me to take his place. But as things stand now, he won't be leaving. Jan has this idea of their moving to a small town, living a more peaceful life."

"The small-town doctors, as I hear them tell it, are hassled as much or more than we are. Of course, Dick does take on a bit more than most of us. Very few doctors will make house calls —"

"He doesn't do a lot of that, but yes — he goes. And I am being trained to do likewise."

"You don't mind?"

"*He* minds. As for me, I only hope I can learn all he can teach me."

"Good boy!" The director went in one direction, Kenneth Harrington in another.

He was undecided. He wanted to contact Dick. Perhaps Foster would attend the afternoon session of the three-day meeting. Kenneth would, but perhaps going to the office the next morning would be his best way to contact his superior. Dick too would need time to get over Jan's disgraceful performance. They might not need to speak of it to each other. Dick would take on the docent program, and Kenny —

Dr. Harrington, the patients said, was a "nice" young man, five years younger than Dick Foster. He was a rather stocky fellow, with smooth black hair and long sideburns which Jan Foster disliked. A dimple would flash in his smooth cheeks, and he was always ready with a smile. Dick Foster had approached him as an assistant in his busy office at a time when Kenny was finishing his second residency in Internal Medicine at General Hospital. He needed help, said Dick; Harrington could try it, and if he liked the job, stay on. To begin, he would be on salary, but within a year he possibly would consider some sort of partnership arrangement. Was Harrington interested?

"I'm in debt for my medical training."

"Anyone like you would be. I've gone through the ropes. You're not married . . ."

"No, sir, I'm not. Probably because of the debt."

"Would you try it?"

"I believe I'd like to try it. You may not like me, you know."

"I've been watching you . . ."

"You watch all the residents."

"That's my job as a staff doctor."

It was, and Foster did his job. Not oppressively goody-goody, just as an honest workman.

Now Kenny had been with him for a year, and he was entirely satisfied with the arrangement. He could not imagine how Foster, or any doctor, could attend such a practice alone. Well, for one thing, he could not take on as many patients. He simply could not.

His offices were well planned to accommodate two doctors, perhaps even three. The suite was in a professional building across a wide street from Research Hospital which was a large, new building, the two upper floors not yet in use. The hospital owned the Doctors' Office Building, and called it a clinic. It scarcely was that, though the occupants did consult when so inclined. But each man's unit was independent.

Dick's had a large waiting room, five examination rooms, three doctor-consultation offices, a small lab, a business area, and a pleasant young woman at the reception desk who held the reins of procedure firmly in her hands. Leslie Jackson, a handsome young woman with a mass of red-gold hair, a bright smile, and a quick tongue. An R.N., she ran the office and the people who worked there. It was to Leslie that Kenneth had expressed his fear that, after his first year, he was not ready to become a partner. Money problems, nothing else. She understood and promised him that Dick would understand. Which he did.

That morning the waiting room was well occupied. The woman who thought she had syphilis was determinedly waiting for Dr. Foster.

"He's at the hospital," said Leslie to Dr. Harrington. "All three at once, I suspect. How did the meeting go?"

Kenneth sat down in the chair beside her and told her how it had gone, keeping his voice low enough that the patients ten feet behind him could not hear. He had felt sorry for Dick, he told Leslie.

"I know. The big lug. Everyone loves him, but —"

"Would you say that Jan loves him?"

Leslie regarded him with wide blue eyes. "Something happened?"

Kenneth told her what had happened. Leslie whistled softly. "What did the doctor do?"

"He said he would be a docent."

"What does this docent thing really mean?"

So Kenny told her, quickly. He should be at work.

"And he didn't kill Jan?"

"Not right there and then. That marriage, Leslie —"

"You asked if Jan loved him. I think she must, Kenny. I think she did when they married — that was in Doctor's intern days. I understand she was a girl from a small town, or farm, maybe a patient, maybe working at the hospital where he trained. Now —"

"Half the people present have heard her say the same thing before — about leaving his city practice, and —"

"Dick . . ."

"No, of course he won't do it. He is a city person, he's built up this office and these patients, and Jan has a lovely home which she keeps like a display area in a furniture store. Everything just so, the windows shining, no dust anywhere. Lemon oil is her favorite perfume."

"But it isn't Dick's."

"He plays square with her, but no, he wants more out of life, and I hope he gets it. Though what a home life it must be, Kenneth!"

Kenneth knew that Leslie did her share to lighten Dick's life. A fact known throughout the office but never discussed or acknowledged.

Dr. Harrington stood up. "I must get to

work. Send in the lady with syphilis . . . and after her —" He looked across the waiting room; all but two of the chairs were occupied. "Maybe we have Jan to thank for the hard work Dick does."

"Maybe we do," said Leslie. "Do you want to take your lady's record with you?" Kenny reached his hand for the file. "Is Dick really going to do this docent thing?" she asked, looking somewhat concerned.

"He's said he would. He'll tell you all about it. But I am sure he will do it."

"And thrive on it. Bye-bye."

Kenneth went back to his office and the "syphilis" patient came in. She told the doctor that she would need only the shot that morning, no tests.

Kenny nodded. "If Dr. Foster thinks you need more —"

"I know. He will call me. And that makes another office call."

Dr. Harrington made no comment, though he was tempted to tell the woman to go home and clear the way —

For an hour he worked hard, the nurses worked hard, the lab buzzed and hummed and clicked. It was the usual run of patients, the arthritic old and the runny-nosed young, a case of shingles with the victim ready to tell the doctor what to do. A backache, inevitably; a man who was going to have to have prostate surgery. And objecting. "Please come back when Dr. Foster is here," said Dr. Harrington pleasantly.

"When will he ever be here?" asked the man who was in pain, with a license to be crabby.

"Call ahead and find out," said Dr. Harrington. "I think you could locate him as early as this afternoon."

"But you ain't sure."

If he were, Kenny would not admit it. Instead he would go down the hall for a cup of coffee. It was eleven o'clock.

He called Leslie on the house phone and told her. Before he hung up he saw Dick Foster parking his car. "Dick's here," he said softly.

"Go get your coffee."

Kenny did, and rested for ten minutes while drinking it. Then he used what the office called the "facilities" and scrubbed his hands. He came out to bump squarely into Dick, who had changed to his white office garments.

"Miss Jackson says you've been busy," said Dick.

Kenny lifted an eyebrow. The staff had its own signs and euphemisms. Patients were so quick to resent a laugh, to misinterpret an overheard comment.

"We spent the morning . . ." Kenny began, then looking beyond Dick, he said, "Oh, oh!" without making a sound.

Dick did not look around; he ducked into his own consultation room; Kenny found shelter in his. Certain patients, those of long standing, became all too familiar with the mechanics and locales of the office setup. They would bypass Leslie at the front desk, come in from the parking lot and knock on a door — even open it.

Tottering down the hall this morning was a small woman, aged, and still pretty. She stretched her hand to the wall to steady herself, and she knocked on Dick's door, then opened it. He looked up from his desk, pushed some papers on it to one side, and rose. He led the woman to the patient's chair, and offered to take her coat.

She drew it close about her. "I am having those dizzy spells again, Dr. Foster," she said in the loud, uninflected voice of the deaf.

"I am sorry," said the doctor. "Are they so bad that —"

"No, I didn't tell my husband I was coming. He doesn't want me to know what is wrong with me."

Dick sighed. "Mrs. Parks," he said, speaking slowly and clearly, "you have been to every doctor in this city, to Mayo's, and specialists all over the country. They have all told you that —"

She folded her white-gloved hands together. "That I have Ménière's disease," she said calmly. "That nothing can be done for it. So I go on being dizzy, and last Sunday — no, two weeks ago — I fell down the steps at church."

Dick closed his eyes for a second. Had she? Possibly. "I didn't know that, Mrs. Parks."

"I twisted my ankle. My husband took me to the hospital — to Research — and they x-rayed it. But they only put an elastic bandage on it."

"A sprain."

"Oh, they said it was. They think there is no use putting my foot in a cast when I have cancer all over my body."

Dick Foster straightened in his chair. "Whatever gave you the idea that you had cancer?" he shouted.

His patient looked pleased with herself. "You doctors kept it from me, didn't you? You thought you did. But I knew. I know. I can read. I have friends who have died of it. I know there is only one thing that gives me the pain I have — that hangs on — You can't operate, so you are not telling me."

Dick leaned back in his chair and regarded the tiny woman in the chair at the corner of his desk. “Mrs. Parks,” he said quietly, “how long have you known me?”

He had to repeat himself, and he did so, patiently. “It’s been a long time,” she agreed. “Ten years?”

“Not quite that long, but you were among my first patients when I entered private practice.”

“I remember when you did that. My daughter worked with the auxiliary, and the women talked about it. They said you were very good.”

Dick laughed. “All right. Who are we to dispute the ladies of the auxiliary? So you’ve been coming to me for various reasons for more than five years.”

“My ears —”

“I know. You have a dreadful disease, and the head noises alone would tip me off my perch.”

“What perch?” she asked brightly. Mrs. Parks had a disconcerting way of always hearing the things irrelevantly said.

He laughed. Dick was big, not bulky. His hair was blond, and well kept, but it often showed the fingers he ran through it in the course of the day. His skin was fresh, and his voice pleasant. He had very blue, very steady blue eyes.

"I said I sympathized entirely with your difficulties because of the Ménière's. It was developed when I first saw you. Of course it affects your nerves, your digestion, and you don't react well to some of the medicines given you."

"You don't give me much!"

"Well, to control the dizziness, to help you sleep — I work in moderation more than the specialists and the clinic doctors you have gone to see."

"You've sent me."

"When asked, yes, I have referred you. I knew what you would be told."

"But you didn't tell them that I had cancer."

Dick sighed and looked at the papers on his desk, the files of at least ten patients, as many pink slips of telephone calls he was supposed to return. He must make some sort of record of what had gone on while he was away for three days, the patients he had seen in the hospitals that morning. He had promised a docent meeting at eight that night. Jan would expect him for dinner.

"You don't have cancer," he said flatly.

"You mean that you won't tell me that I have."

"You have gone to a dozen other doctors. Have they . . . ?"

"No, because you tell them not to. You've told my husband and son not to tell me."

Dick stood up. "Mrs. Parks," he said patiently, "I am going to take you out to your car. Please rest until this spell of dizziness goes away. I do wish you would arrange a downstairs bedroom so that you won't have any more falls."

"You haven't looked at my ankle."

"No. You said the emergency room at Research had cared for that. It will get well."

"I am going to a cancer specialist."

He was not surprised. "Which one?"

"I won't tell you, nor Parks, nor my son. Then you can't caution him not to tell me."

"That's all right, if you go to see a reputable man. I'd hate to have a less than able one get hold of you."

"I'll take care of myself. All right, I'll leave. You have other things to do."

He did. One of them was to call Mrs. Parks' son and warn him.

He came back to his desk and tried to make some sort of orderly program for himself and the rest of the afternoon. He would answer the urgent telephone calls, he would see the patients for whom Leslie had made appointments, he would —

Sometime he must get food into his big,

hungry body. There would be coffee and cans of instant things in the lounge, but not the food and the half hour of relaxation one should have while eating.

He went to work, once encountering Kenny in the hall. "Did you have a busy morning?" he asked.

Kenny nodded. "I did. People who wanted to see you, and besides that two pregnancies and one abortion."

Dick's head turned sharply.

"Oh," said Kenny quietly. "I told her that we didn't perform any sort of surgery. Being so close to Research and all, we couldn't possibly do abortions."

Dick laughed and nodded. "If they bought that —"

"They didn't. I think I lost us about five patients today."

"And out of the five . . ."

"Yes, sir. One made a row."

"That figures. I had a little problem of my own." And he told about Mrs. Parks and her "cancer." "You would think that what she does have would be enough."

"You're being assigned your docents to-night, aren't you?"

"If I can get home for dinner, and Jan lets me out again. I am on my way for a Sego now. Join me?"

"Leslie brought me a sandwich when she went to lunch. She decided that you would have eaten before coming back to the zoo."

"I wish she had told me," said Dick, and he went on toward the lounge.

Kenny went to the door of the waiting room and asked Miss Jackson if he could see her for a minute.

"Is anything wrong?" Leslie asked, following Kenny into an examination room.

"Our boss is drinking instant breakfast and planning a day that would kill a normal man. Besides, it seems that he has to go home for dinner before he attends the docent meeting."

Leslie ran her hand up under her thick hair. "Can we do anything?" she asked.

"Not without infuriating Jan Foster, and probably Dick as well."

"Why does he have to go home for dinner?"

"I suppose he promised to."

"Sea kelp and broiled sunflower seed."

"Is she still on that kick?"

"I don't really know. She can cook. She keeps a beautiful home. But she grabs every fad that the newspapers give room to."

"And tonight . . . ?"

"I don't think she will poison him, but she will make every effort to keep him from attending that meeting."

"I think — I was with him, you know — I think he might have refused the docent assignment if she had stayed at home or kept quiet at the meeting."

"Will it add to his work?"

"Yes."

"We can refuse patients."

Kenny turned his head. "You like to live dangerously, don't you?"

"Then our only chance is that Jan will prevent his taking that on."

"She says she is going to do just that. Tonight she will make her try."

"On her cooking?" Leslie let herself indulge in some raunchy descriptions of Jan Foster's food ideas.

Kenny laughed, even as he clicked his tongue reprovingly against the roof of his mouth.

"I'm sorry," said Leslie, "but there are times, and this is one of them, when I could kill that woman."

"I wouldn't if I were you. The homicide squad always suspects the other woman first."

She laughed, and went to look at herself in the mirror and smooth her hair.

"I think," said Kenny, his hand on the doorknob, "that our only hope is to make things as easy here as we can for the old man."

He opened the door in the face of Dick Foster, who had heard the final words.

"Who's old?" he asked. He had a handful of crackers which he was eating, one by one.

"You are," said Kenny. "You're a docent, full of years, knowledge and experience."

"That only makes me feel old," Dick said, reaching for the report sheet which the technologist had ready for him. "I am not, really," he explained. "And the ladies know that I am not." He winked broadly at the lab girl who giggled, then he turned to kiss Leslie's cheek as he walked past her.

The three he left behind had been taken completely by surprise. "Hey, Doc," Kenny called after him. "You should watch your b.p."

"I think you'll find it pretty good for an old man," said Dick, turning into his office. He closed the door firmly behind himself. Kenny made a shooing gesture to the still astonished technologist, and touched Leslie's arm. "You won't need to kill Janice," he said thoughtfully. "I think our boss is about ready to do the job himself."

Dick knew only that he was feeling tired. More tired than he ordinarily would have been at this time on a Monday. The docent meeting was to blame, he knew that, but he didn't want to take the matter out and study it. Jan — his home — his whole life — he did not often examine or assess those things. He knew that they had fouled up for him. There were those who asked why he did not divorce Jan. "I don't have grounds," was his reply. "She keeps my home, she accepts her marital duties. And — she won't divorce me."

But what about Leslie? "Leslie knows her status, too. She can boss me now, a little. We are good friends. Married, she would have to leave the office and stay out of my affairs."

"Do you love her?"

"Physically, we respond to each other. Maybe we do love each other, and maybe someday —" Meaning, but not spoken of, was the ever-possible death of her husband, an invalid.

Meanwhile, things stayed as they were. And Dick worked too hard. Life was not all it should be, and he knew that better than anyone. But he did mean to keep his medical affairs the most important part of his life, and in order. That had been an unstated promise he had made to himself.

He reached for the notes and the reports which Leslie had stacked on his desk. Pushing the mail aside, he spent a second deciding whether to make the requested telephone calls or dictate his notes on the morning's activities, his work at the three hospitals. The big City General where he enjoyed the variety of cases and the frank and open way those people could and did express themselves. "I feel like hell, Doc," was the sort of response he would get from a man gasping for breath.

Children's was fun — sometimes. Sometimes killing tragedy. But he liked that hospital, too. The little girl with a new doll to show him, the boy who always must listen to the doctor's heart.

He reached for the recording mouthpiece, snapped the switch and began to talk. He leaned back in his chair as he did this, and looked through the bare, uncurtained part of the window up at the bulk of Research. A big, new hospital, too big it was beginning to seem. The upper two floors were unused, though kept in condition, elevators running, electric lights and gadgets operative.

He frowned and leaned forward. He had seen something move behind one of the blank windows. No one was supposed — Well, maybe a janitor dusting things off. Yes! That would be it. But the janitors at Research wore olive drab shirts and trousers. Dick had seen a flash of white. Maybe he'd ask Sister about the people who might be up there.

He went on talking into the tape recorder. Finished, he picked up the schedule which Leslie had put on his desk. Five patients, one at least was going to need hospitalization and tests — that one would take up time, and time to protest, argue —

Sighing, he put the schedule down. Looked at the mail and the pink slips that would require phone calls. Sighing again — no wonder, all morning, people had been telling him that he looked tired. Well, he felt tired. He pushed a button, and Leslie answered. "Yes, sir?" All proper and correct.

"Do I really have to see the Bannisters today, Les?"

"They are waiting, Doctor."

He groaned. "I'm swamped."

"Yes, Doctor."

"Would you please get my brother on the phone, dear?" He knew that he should tell Gene about the docent thing before he could read it in the newspaper. Gene often felt left out of things, suspecting that he was being "saved." Which he was. But in his place, Dick would resent it, too. "Don't buzz me until you have him on the horn," he said aloud to Leslie. "These executives put on airs."

Laughter trembled in Leslie's voice. "I do

the same for you, Doctor. I ask callers to hold."

Leslie laughed, and so did he, and he put the phone down, feeling better. He could *talk* to Leslie!

He went back to work, making some notes, reading former ones, on the Bannister case. He was going to send those people to a gynecologist whether they wanted to go or not. Of course they wanted children! So did their doctor. But to implant the husband's sperm into a healthy, young, and strange woman — They even wanted Dick to find that woman. She must not have a boy friend; she must be blond, with blue eyes, of European ancestry. She must live in their home from the time of insemination until proven pregnant.

Artificial insemination with a female carrier was rare; Dick had explained that they were asking someone to undertake the risk of pregnancy, and then give up the child. Mrs. Bannister said the reason for the search was that her husband wanted to carry on his bloodline and have an heir.

"Kooks!" said Dick firmly. "I couldn't start out my virgin docent students on a case like that." He grinned at himself, and made a note on the letter which he had been reading while he thought about the Bannisters. Of course he was sorry for people who wanted children and couldn't have them, just as he pitied the ones that had children and didn't want them.

Jan could have children, but Dick had stopped wanting her to have his. She would not make a good mother. Gene — It was taking Leslie a time to locate his brother. Dick tipped his head back on his shoulders and thought about Gene. Twelve years older than Dick Foster, Gene had married only five years ago, and then to a woman of forty. But they had a good life together. Gene had known Marlene for years. She had been his "girl."

Now she was forty-five; they had been married for five years, and she made a good life for Gene. They traveled; they had a warm home, but a newspaper left beside a chair, a used glass standing on the kitchen sink, was no crime for Marlene.

They lived next door to Dick. He and his brother had built the two houses eight — ten? — years ago. Similar, not alike. But both were fine houses. Dick's of white brick, Gene's of red. Two-storied, with a good lawn space, tall trees and flower beds. They jointly hired a gardener who worked there with the understanding that Mrs. Gene Foster was to tell him what to do.

The houses stood in the lee of a wooded

hill. They had no very close neighbors, but the road which led to them was well-maintained. Gene's business dealt with the sale of heavy road machinery, and snow never clogged the doctor's driveway.

"You don't appreciate the service," Gene told Dick.

"You get your doctoring free, don't you?"

They were close, those brothers. Marlene came from a large family. She had several sisters, a brother or two. Some of these had families of their own; they visited, and brought children into Gene's house, into the yard. Gene enjoyed that, and Dick most certainly did. He laid out a tennis court, against Jan's wishes, and was talking about a swimming pool.

This would have already been accomplished, except —

Gene came on the phone, making Dick jump. "Where the devil were you?" he shouted.

Gene answered delicately. "In the bathroom, if you must know."

Dick chuckled. "How are you?" he asked.

Three years ago, Gene had suffered a heart attack. With Dick's close eye upon him, he had recovered, but he also slowed down about fifty per cent on his activities. Marlene watched him, too. He spent fewer hours in the office; they attended no large parties. She watched his diet and his exercise. And again they spoke of a pool. Swimming would be good for Gene.

Dick told his brother that he was busy, but he wanted Gene to know. "You tell Marlene before she gets Jan's version."

"I don't think they are speaking at the moment."

That happened. Some nephew ran over a petunia bed, a niece was impudent. As she probably had been, kids being what they were.

So Dick told Gene about the docent thing.

"What are you striking for?" asked the older man. "Two hearts in the family? Because I judge you are going to do it."

"I was inclined to decline — I know I am too busy. But Jan decided it for me."

"What was she doing there?"

"Making decisions for me."

"So you accepted. Are you really going to do it?"

"Yes. If I can. But really not to spite Jan. I'd enjoy doing it. It would be a new thing and exciting. If we ever get our medical school —"

"Could you cut down somewhere else?"

"I have to work to be a teaching example."

"Not with your tongue hanging out."

Dick laughed. "I'll watch that, if I do it.

Leslie will watch it. And I myself know that I am busy enough, but I really would like to help those students; maybe I can get some more primaries for the city. Primaries are G.P.'s, buddy."

"You're not enough for this city?" teased Gene.

"Well, not really."

"So what's wrong?"

Dick's eyebrows went up. "Need there be anything wrong?"

"No, I suppose not. But you keep saying 'if.' What would happen, what would you do, *if*—"

"I hate to take on another battle with Jan."

He could hear Gene talking to himself. And he could guess the context. But when Gene spoke clearly, it was to ask, quite calmly, "Does she have a reason?"

"That I am too busy to take on anything else. The thing that bugged me was that she came to the meeting."

"Were wives . . . ?"

"How many wifelike things does Jan do? How many non-wifelike? The point is she was there, and she spoke up in the meeting. When my name was announced as one of the docents, she stood up and told the medics present that I could not accept. That I was too busy."

He was silent for a second, remembering how Jan had looked, and how she had spoken.

Gene was swearing again. "I can just see her," he told Dick. "Sitting like a Buddha, listening, and finally pronouncing — Dick, I would not put up with it —"

"You wouldn't, maybe, but I seem to have to. Of course I told the committee that I approved the plan, and that I would serve. Tonight I am to meet my students."

"And go on living with Jan."

Dick laughed, though weakly. "That seems to be the situation I have to live with."

"At least, you do live with it. I hope nothing has happened to Leslie."

"Nothing has," said Dick, his laughter coming more freely. "And I suspect, on that note, that we had better hang up. I surely don't want a scandal in the office. Yours or mine. Though for a doctor, it is especially bad."

"Huh!" said Gene. "I've not known it to bother you before. And I hope it won't now. I'd like to see you make it worse."

They both hung up, and Dick went to work. He would rather not be late for dinner, since he had every intention of attending the docent meeting, and being on time for it.

He did attend, and he did meet his six students. They looked him over; he studied them and talked briefly with each one. A mixed bag, but the other men had the same, judging from appearances.

From now on he would attend only to his own group, work out a program — and speculate as little as possible about how Jan would treat each one when the time came for the docent to live in the doctor's home for a few weeks.

There was some open discussion; Dick was anxious to get home and to bed. When speaking to each student, he got telephone numbers and names, the primary medical interests, if any, of each student, and said that they would hear from him. He found himself inclined to like some individuals more than others. "Cut it out, Foster," he chided himself. He was not, himself, so far removed from medical school that he did not know one could not judge from appearances. Not much, anyway. He had one black, he had one woman — the others, well, except for the smoothie who "had his own car, thank you, Doctor" — these young folk wanted to be doctors, and presumably would work hard to make medical school.

He should have found out their class schedules, but he could get them from the college office. He had better clear his mind for a good night's sleep. He had promised Sister, Administrator of Research, to see her at eight the next day. And, parking his car, going into the house, he remembered the shadowy figure he had seen, or thought he had seen, at the window of the top floor of that hospital. The empty floor. He could ask Sister.

He went into the silent house, back to the kitchen for a glass of milk, then, having checked door locks, upstairs. Jan's voice floated from her darkened bedroom. "The small guest room is ready," she said.

"I'll tell you when that is needed," Dick answered.

Jan made no reply, and he went into his own room, the master bedroom, the bed turned down, the towels folded exactly. Jan was an exquisite housekeeper. He took a shower and got into bed. ". . . won't need to plan. Let 'em tag along whatever I am doing, and I seldom know," he told himself.

He immediately went to sleep, was up at seven, ate the breakfast which Jan had provided; she was about somewhere, but not talkative.

Sister Alphonsus was. She had a problem. Tact and some detective work was needed. "And you can't handle it?" Dick asked gallantly.

She smiled patiently. "My handling becomes immediately evident. I need a spy."

"Me?" Dick was honestly surprised.

"Well, I am told that on one of the payrolls there are two names of people who don't work in the surgical business office. I think I know most of the personnel . . . But the Chief says he doesn't know these two people."

"Cut their names off the payroll and they'll surface. Or be proven to be ghosts."

She smiled widely. Sister still wore her coronet and habit. She was ready to try new things in the hospital. For herself — "I knew you'd be the one to help," she said.

"That's me all over," said Dick. "My wife told me this morning that I thought I knew it all."

"Doesn't she think you do?"

"You've never met my wife?"

"I should like to sometime."

"Ah-huh," said Dick. "Have you heard about the docent program?"

"I read about it in last night's newspaper. Do you have some interesting students?"

"I hope so. I've just barely met them. They seem exactly like the people I went to pre-med with. I'll be trailing them about, so you'll see. Now I must — Oh, Sister!"

"Yes, Doctor?"

"Does anyone use the rooms on the top of this building?"

"Oh, no. They get dusted out each Thursday, but —"

"Then I saw a ghost yesterday. A live ghost in your hospital, Sister!" He tried to sound stern, but his eyes always twinkled.

"You need to get some rest, Doctor," said the Administrator.

"I will, one of these days. Now I am going to throw the floor nurses into a tizzy by making rounds all among the baths and the breakfast trays."

She waved him on, even as she reached for the telephone.

"Ghosts in the attic," Dick said to himself, going toward the elevator. "Ghosts on Surgery's payroll. And I do hope this diabetic will agree to give up sugar."

Chapter 2

Within six months the docent program was going full strength. Not without incidents, not without hitches. Within the first week, Dick had enlisted Kenny as partner in the project. It was to be a joint affair, with credit for both working on it.

"If we're any good," said Kenny.

"What comparative reference do we have? I suppose the thing is operative elsewhere, but here in this city, can't you and I equal Truesdell? Utley doesn't worry me. He's lost one of his, so he has only five."

"Did he leave pre-med?"

"I don't know. I think it was need for a part-time job."

"Wellinghof talks about money."

"I know he does. I put him onto applying for a student loan."

But the docent program was working. Assignments were made, and usually kept. Nicknames flourished. "Little Doc. Big Doc."

Dick had known and used the same when he was in medical school.

Some patients were overzealous about the students, some objected strenuously to having one in the examination room or trailing the doctor when he made hospital rounds. Some ignored them.

The students worried, too. "I think Crans and McDonald are bored," Kenny decided.

"Leslie says Rogers would make a pass at her or any of the office girls."

"I'll believe that. Alice Baus is on the eager-beaver side."

"I talked to her about that, and she said a woman medic had to be."

"She could be right. How do you like Leroy?"

"Wellinghof? I think of him as Uriah Heep. And that is a handicap."

"Harold Jackson is poor, too. But he demands his rights, and seems to resent the tuition students."

"Twenty years ago, black men attended medical schools, and some of them became good doctors. Today, I suppose the results will be the same."

"Quotas," mused Kenny. "Personally, I don't think that system is all good."

"Well, of course it can be good. But, with Jackson at least, we seem to be off on the wrong foot. He looks to his color to help him, not his ability. And that's a waste. If he would work, he'd do the job. Maybe not a brilliant job, but don't forget, under any system, half of our practicing doctors were not in the top half of their class at med school. But I can't tell him that, or Jan. She unfortunately, takes his side, and thinks she is helping him. Helping the poor, she'd call it."

"She may be sorry."

"You bet. They watched *Roots* together, and Jackson offered an argument when I got called to a gall bladder."

"But you took him."

"I took him, and he stayed with me when I took the woman to the hospital. But I think he learned one thing that night. He asked me why I argued with the patient. You know? I asked her why she would endure such terrific pain, when comparatively simple surgery, et cetera, et cetera. Jackson asked me why I didn't just order her to have the surgery."

"And you told him . . ."

"Driving home, I did. Then he got off on Reed Crans, said he wanted to be on hand when Crans took his turn at Neighborhood House."

"Will he be?"

"I won't plan for it. Crans is older, he has a degree, he drives a good car, and wears good clothes. Jackson knows he has the money he needs but has no idea of how rich the guy's family is."

"What would he do if he did know?"

"I think Crans can handle anything. I admire him for wanting to study medicine."

"But why here? Why in this school which is still a figment?"

"I believe there is a girl."

"Oh, well, then!"

Dick laughed. "Are we making progress?"

"I believe so. Truesdell doesn't think we are. Utley is beginning to brag a bit."

"Mhmmmn. Are you asking for conclusions from the students you take on?"

"I've begun to. Alice Baus argues."

"I know she does. Well — here comes Jackson."

"What patients do you have?"

"The usual, but there is a woman who wants to live on PVM, and a man I am sure has an abdominal aneurysm."

"Good Lord. Maybe I should sit in, too."

"I'll step aside."

Kenny went down the hall, and Dick greeted Jackson, who came into the room and sat down in the corner. Dick pointed his pencil at the white coat on the rack, and Jackson put it on. "You pay too much attention to little things, Doc," he said.

"That could be. It keeps me busy."

Leslie brought him his appointment cards, and the record folders, nodded to Jackson and said "Hi!" pleasantly. Jackson stared at her, and said nothing.

"Send in the first one," Dick told her.

As he did with every patient, Dick gave Jackson a brief summary of the case. This first one was a child with a bad cold. When they entered, "This is Melvin," he said, "and his mother, Mrs. Abernathy. How are you, Mother? I can see how Melvin is. Have you met Jackson; he is a pre-medical student, and one of my docent observers. He is here to watch, listen, and learn."

"And catch Melvin's cold," said Melvin's mother. "He gets so many of them, Dr. Foster."

"I know he does. I am beginning to wonder if they are all colds. Would you consider taking him to an allergist?"

"Are they expensive?"

"Oh, we're all expensive. But there are clinics. I could refer you."

"We don't need *free* care."

"I know that, and a specialist would be better. He'd adjust his rates to your ability to pay, and if he helped Melvin, you would save my bills."

There was a little more talk. Dick examined the child and called an allergist for an appointment for Melvin Abernathy. He wiped the child's nose and gave him a small packet of tissues. "You can't get rich doin' that way, Doc," Jackson told him, watching the child and woman depart.

"I'm not interested in getting rich. Are you?"

"I have to be. I'm at school on Government money; they want us blacks scattered around."

Dick ignored the declaration and buzzed for the next patient. He could have that discussion with Kenny, but not yet with the tall, good-looking black man who was spoiling for a fight.

He made notes and Jackson ignored his suggestion that the student also keep a record.

"Why?" said the tall young man in his white coat.

"If you plan to practice medicine . . ."

"I'll be a doctor, if that's what you mean. No new medical school is going to start out by firing its minority students."

Dick sighed. "Oh, Harold Jackson," he said, "you accuse the whites of discrimination, and yet you lean on the fact that you are black, and different!"

Jackson shrugged. "We are going to make it."

"The only blacks I know who have really made it on a level with the whites were ready to do it by digging in and working for what they wanted. They wasted little time telling us that they were good enough; they showed us."

Jackson made no comment, and Dick silently rebuked himself for breaking his own rule of arguing with the man. "This is a big case," he said quietly.

It was a big case. The man, in his seventies, a retired military officer, had had lung surgery five years before; the cancer not recurring. A week ago he had come to Dr. Foster to say he was not well; he occasionally had pain in his chest — maybe his stomach — and Dick had sent him to Research for tests. For some reason the man did not want to avail himself of the military hospital service. Now the doctor must tell the distinguished gentleman that an aneurysm had been detected on the aorta — stopping, and using a chart of the human body to explain both to the patient and to the student what an aneurysm was and where this one had been discovered — in a position that made surgery impossible.

"I wish they would try," said the officer.

"It would mean immediate death, sir."

"I don't think I'll like living in constant fear."

"No, you won't like it."

"Is there any chance . . . ?"

"Only a slim one, but of course life always holds hope. You must avoid strenuous activities —"

"No golf?"

"I wouldn't advise long tee shots. You can walk, but don't jog. You can swim, but don't dive. A cocktail or highball with your dinner, a diet you know will agree with you. No heavy lifting."

The patient rose to his feet. "How will I know . . ."

"Usually an aneurysm breaks without warning, but I am always available if there are symptoms, bleeding — perhaps discomfort. If it would help, come here regularly for me to check your general condition."

"This, sir, is a shock —"

"Yes. It was to me as well."

"My wife —"

"I'll be glad to talk to her about it."

"Yes. Yes."

The man departed. "He's sure shook," said Jackson.

"So am I," said Dick.

"This doctor business — seems to me you hurt as often as you help."

"Not really. Our being a doctor doesn't change the fact of a broken leg, or, as in this case, an incurable condition, but the patient, not informed on the matter, counts on us to do what we can. Do you understand?"

"If 'twas me, I'd shoot myself and get it over."

"That's one way out," Dick agreed. "The general won't take it. He's been a very brave man, and he is deeply religious —"

"That don't do him any good now."

"I think it will. Let's take up the next patient."

"Dr. Foster?"

"Yes, Jackson?"

"If I was in that man's shoes, I reckon I'd be glad to know a doctor like you. You gave it to him straight, and you showed you cared."

Well, for Pete's sake!

"I do care, Jackson. And I am trying to teach you fellows what it means to care."

"Yes, sir."

Late that afternoon, Dick told Kenny what had been done and said. "D'you think we're doing something right?" he asked.

"Sometimes we are. Is Jackson at class now?"

"Yes. He's with me for the rest of the week. Jan treats him like the Sultan of Zulu."

"Truesdell asked me if we thought it was

safe to take these characters into our homes."

"What did he have in mind?"

"Who knows, with Truesdell? I think burglary was the farthest he'd gone by then."

"With rape to follow. Mhmmmn. We do have a lot of things to think about, don't we?"

"Go home. You've had a day."

Dick did go home, immediately changing into some old chino slacks and a T-shirt so that he could work with his roses. He had two hobbies: one indoor, one out. His two rose beds, three tree roses, four trellises on which he trained climbers, were his out-of-doors recreation. Indoors, mainly during the winter, and using a workshop in the basement of the house, he made miniature furniture, exquisite copies of museum pieces, of cameos, of tiny rugs and carpets. His skill was great, and his patience infinite. Because he was successful in both ventures, he was relieved of the all-day pressures of his profession.

This evening he spent an hour with his roses — cutting off dead blossoms, loosening dirt, setting a soaker hose — and came in to dinner, cleaned up and calm.

He spent the evening reading and went to bed early. Jackson watched TV with Jan. Gene was all right. He had come out to talk to his brother for ten minutes while Dick worked with the roses. So the doctor could go to bed with a clear conscience, the phone had not rung one single time.

But, ten minutes after midnight, it did ring. Before answering, Dick sat up in bed and put his bare feet on the floor.

He answered, he listened, then he crossed the hall and shook Jackson awake. "We have to go out," he said.

"Me too?"

Dick did not answer that. "I can dress in five minutes," he said.

Jackson could not, but he was ready to slide into the car as Dick backed it out of the garage. "You remember to tell your wife where you goin'?" he asked.

"I'll call the answering service from the house."

"We goin' to a house?"

"Yes. This woman is a patient, and has been for years. Her family — she has five children —"

"You know what's wrong?"

"Her daughter said severe stomach pains."

"Another baby?"

"No." Dick drove steadily.

"These rich people?"

"The husband is a bricklayer; he employs other —"

"That can be rich."

"Not with five children and a well-used Bourbon bottle."

"Wife drink too?"

"Some. Not to excess."

They had reached their destination. A low, red-brick house, with the light on above the front door, and the daughter waiting.

Their patient was in the bedroom, limp with pain. Yes, she had been sick for several days, and sicker —

"Why didn't you bring her to me earlier?" Dick asked, his large clean hands feeling the distended abdomen.

"Mamma wouldn't let us."

"I could have had tests made. Now — Where's the telephone?"

"What —"

"I am calling an ambulance. I am taking her to the hospital. Where's your dad?"

He'd gone somewhere.

"When he comes in, if he's able, send him to Research Hospital. I'll need someone to sign your mother in." Yes, the oldest daughter could go along.

"The ambulance will scare her," said Jackson.

"I'm scared myself," said the doctor bluntly.

He called Research and gave a sedative to

the patient; she was a very sick woman. As they drove to the hospital, he explained the case to Jackson.

He talked about abdominal conditions. He suspected this case would involve the intestines, and peritonitis would be inevitable.

"Will they cut?"

Dick drew his eyebrows together. "Get rid of that word," he advised. "It's nonprofessional. Yes, we'll do surgery."

"I ain't goin' to watch."

"Oh, yes, you are —" said the doctor firmly. "From the observer balcony. But you'll watch. Or your medical career won't ever get off the ground."

Jackson said nothing, and Dick did not pursue the matter. He parked at his usual place at his office. He unlocked doors and went inside to get the patient's record. The ambulance was still in the emergency entrance of the hospital across the street. He glanced up at the top floors of Research as he left the office. "That's become a habit with me," he said aloud.

He told Jackson to follow him, and went across the road. "Sure spooky up there at night," said Jackson.

Dick nodded. At the moment, he had more important things to do than think about spooks. "Stay close," he told Jackson.

"Patient admission on an emergency basis is sometimes complicated."

He talked to the surgical resident, he talked to Maria Pollack, his patient. They would take care of her, he said.

"Surgery?" she asked weakly.

Dick smiled down at her. "I've been warning you."

She knew that he had.

He did not mention the peritonitis to her, but he talked of it extensively to the doctors, in Jackson's hearing. He had explained the tall young man's presence. He was not a medical student. Pre-med only. "But I am his docent and have promised that he can observe."

This was arranged, family consent was given, Maria Pollack had her surgery — a tumor discovered on her intestines — the peritonitis made the situation critical, drains were placed, and the patient moved to Intensive Care.

It was five in the morning when Dick could tell Jackson they would leave for home.

"We'll stop for some breakfast."

"I can whup up some bacon and eggs."

Dick shook his head. "Not in my wife's kitchen; she frowns on outside help."

"Ain't you the boss?"

"Yes, and I do what pleases my wife."

Jackson made a grunting sound of disapproval. "That ain't a part of my learnin' doctorin'?"

"Oh, no. Now ask me any questions you have. When's your first class?"

"Eight A.M."

"All right. Call the office to locate me or Dr. Harrington."

"You two in on this together?"

"We are."

"Doctors usually do that way?"

"Not often as closely and completely as Harrington and I do. We are especially compatible. So what he tells you comes from me."

"That compatible thing — I wouldn't like it. I won't ever get myself married on account of that! Miss Jan — your wife — does she like this compatible thing with your partner?"

"Not for the first time, I must tell you that we won't discuss Mrs. Foster."

But of course Jackson knew. Dick supposed everyone knew. He wished things were different, but a man could not have everything — in a marriage, in a business partnership. He was well aware that Kenny and Jan heartily disliked each other. Kenny said nothing to that effect; Jan said everything.

Loudly, and abroad. She may even have talked about it to his docent pupil. He would follow the laid-out plan of not discussing personal matters with his student; standing back and watching must tell him enough.

He dropped Jackson at the university, and went on to his office. He would have time to tape the events of the night. He did this, shaved, and went across to Research to make rounds and see how Maria Pollack was doing. Her family, frightened, clustered around him. He held up his hand. "Wait, wait," he admonished. "I've just come in myself."

Maria, he decided, would probably make it, but she was a sick woman; the peritonitis would get worse before it got better. He must watch it carefully. He wrote his orders, and slipped into the stairwell rather than go out to the elevators and past the waiting room. Cowardly, but he had nothing to tell the family. Besides, the surgeon was really in charge.

The office was beginning to come to life. It still was early. But Leslie was there, first on the telephone which she waved toward Dick in greeting, then with her records and whatever she used to keep the two doctors busy and progressing, the office running smoothly.

"Were you up all night?" she asked when she brought his schedule back to Dick.

"Better than half of it." He mentioned Maria Pollack's surgery. "I wish she had let us do an exploratory last year."

"Not good?"

"We doctors have found a new word."

"Yes, I know. Guarded. You've seen her this morning?"

"Ten minutes ago. Jackson and I had breakfast, and I dropped him at the U."

"How's he doing?"

"So-so. All you Jacksons talk too much."

She ignored his teasing. "Did he go into surgery?"

"Only to observe. But I'll bet he slept through some of it."

"I'd bet on your side."

"When he shows up around noon, switch him to Kenny. He doesn't care about our office arrangement, and he must learn that arrangements are necessary, that they have to be made."

"But Kenny's good to him."

"He doesn't approve of my arrangements at home, either. Jackson, I mean."

"Does he say so?"

"He had better not."

"How do he and Jan make it?"

"Do I have to talk about Jan this morning?"

"No, Doctor, of course not. Does he know that Kenny and Jan hate each other? It might —"

"Hate is a strong word, dear."

"I can find stronger ones. What did or didn't Jan do this morning?"

"Nothing. Literally nothing. I took Jackson to breakfast at a coffee shop; he said, or thought more loudly, that Jan should be serving us bacon and eggs."

"Well, shouldn't she?"

"It would be a bad start for today." Dick looked at his watch.

"You have a half hour," Leslie told him. "I'll get you some coffee."

"Please don't. At ten I have a lecture to listen to at General. I want to sleep."

"You go right to it. Jackson asked me, you know, how you and Jan happened to be married to each other."

Dick sighed. "And you told him that it was none of his business?"

"No. Not in so many words, but I remember what I said when Kenny asked me. In fact, I have a little speech I make whenever I am asked that."

Dick's attention sparked.

"Do people often ask . . . ?"

"Oh, not half as often as they wonder silently."

"Leslie . . ." He sounded and looked helpless. She stretched a hand out to him, but did not touch him. They each believed in, and practiced, a complete separation between their personal and professional relationships.

"I tell people who do ask," she said simply, "that you were married when you were an intern."

Yes. He thought of those hard-working, lonely days and months and years. He thought of the small, dark-haired girl who worked in the hospital offices. She would go with him for coffee, she would listen when he talked. With him, she would walk back to her tiny apartment, and one night he went upstairs with her; the single room was clean, there was a couch — he had spent the night. He could not remember Jan from that one night, though he could clearly see himself, a yellow-haired, rosy-cheeked youth, twenty-five years old, tired, hungry for the things his studies denied him. Jan told that they had met at a party and had gone to bed. . . .

There had been no party. It was too dreary, their primary encounter. But Jan had said that, because of it, they must marry. She was not the sort of girl —

And she was not. Sex never had meant that much to her, even after she had the papers she thought were required, and during the years that followed Jan was content to keep house; Dick was engrossed in building his career. Both had been at fault.

Of course people knew that they were mismatched. They guessed at what might be the truth. Did it matter? The truth. Who cared, anyway? Not Jan, certainly. She got the home she wanted, and kept it perfectly. She joined the League of Women Voters; she welcomed women's lib with open arms . . .

Kenny deplored the whole setup. And he told Jan as much. "The man is being cheated, you know."

"You told me that he had a mistress," Jan said coolly. "Isn't that enough to satisfy him?"

"If I thought you were as ignorant as you pretend . . ." Kenny had been shocked.

"I've never made any trouble about Leslie Jackson."

"I wish you would."

"Because you think Dick would choose sides with Leslie."

"I know he would. Why don't you find out?"

"They'd never be married."

"Maybe not, but Dick would then be free to find a girl who would make him the wife he deserves."

There were many clashes between Jan and Kenny. She could not see why Dick should be late for dinner, or go out on a night call when he had an assistant. "Partner." Even Dick would remind her of that.

"All right. Show me the records that say you do only half of the work."

That was where Dick stood firm. Jan did not come to the office. Jan did not see his records of work, income, or anything pertaining to his professional life.

"What would she do with them, do you suppose?" Leslie once asked Kenny.

"She won't step over the line. She doesn't want a divorce."

"Neither does Dick."

"He will if the right girl comes over the hill."

"Then I pray for the day. I'd miss him, but I do wish he could have a full life."

And she would be left with a paraplegic husband in a Veterans Hospital, a man whom she would never divorce.

"It's all a mess," said Kenny, sounding desperate.

"It is a mess. The trouble is, and your friend Jan knows this, the people involved have principles. Don't ever acquire any, Kenneth, dear."

"Oh, I shan't. But could you bear to see

Dick happily married to another woman?"
"Yes, I could. I love him that much."
"Good girl!"
She laughed. "Not many people call me that!"
Jan and the student would have told the story differently, and probably did. "This Doc, you know, he got a wife who don't want no part of bein' a wife. This Doc ain't one to beat a woman, so he makes out with a chick that works in his office. I reckon he don't care about havin' children, so they get along."
It was Kenny who thought poorly of the whole arrangement. And he, personally, would do all he could to change things for Dick, whom he admired. "I love that man!" he would tell anyone.
Dick knew only that Kenny worked hard and did what Dr. Foster asked of him. For three months he had been married to a plain girl who laughed a lot, and a child now was expected.
Dick was well aware of the war between Jan and Kenny, but he handled that by almost never asking Kenny to his home. Or so he thought. With the office out of bounds for Jan, things should be, at least, contained. And Dick could pay full attention to his office, his work, his roses.

He scarcely ever took notice of anything that developed between Kenny and Jan. Heaven knew that troubles enough bobbed to the surface without digging for them. He even told himself to quit looking up at the blank windows of Research. If something odd was going on there, he need not get into it. Just now he had a lecture, his kind, to give to Claudia, one of the technicians, for the scolding she had given poor little Mrs. Parks about coming into the office through the parking lot door.

He had a lot of work to get through — in the office, in the three hospitals, his office hours, a house call or two. Meetings, consultations. Being a "primary" doctor, he must call in, and work with, specialists, such as surgeons. Maria Pollack had taken a dislike to hers. But there still were neurologists, dermatologists — men who lived in worlds of their own and presumably had their own troubles.

But he could laugh at himself on the day the O.B. man he worked with begged him to try to persuade a new mother not to name her little girl Tearose. "You can't win that kind of row," he told the other man.

"I got 'em to stop naming their babies for me."

"All right then. Quit while you're ahead."

Now he was into the docent thing which should have meant little extra work if he did it the way Truesdell did it, and maybe Utley. But Truesdell had been named director of the project, and he kept calling "evaluation" meetings. There was one arranged for late that afternoon. Each man was asked to report on his progress with his students.

"How long a report?" Dick asked. "If you would do yours first, Truesdell, Utley and I would know what you wanted. Otherwise, this meeting could last all night, or end quickly. You show us the way."

He glanced at Utley, who nodded, his tongue in his cheek. Dick's attention quickened. He must not let something whiz by without noticing it. He listened to Truesdell, who dealt in personalities more often than he did in medical interest or advance. There were only two, he answered a question put by Utley, who "at that point in time" he would consider adequate quality for medical school.

Dick stirred in his chair. "May I say something?" he said.

"Sure," said Utley.

"I think sticking to procedure . . ." Truesdell began.

"I was just wondering if personalities were too much our affair. The school knew whom they were putting into the docent program. It is natural that we would like some of the candidates better than others, personally."

"You are able to maintain the impersonal attitude?" Truesdell asked coldly.

"I do my best. There are all sorts of graduated and practicing M.D.'s. Why shouldn't the average be the same for students?"

"Perhaps we can weed out the unfortunate personalities in the training program," suggested Truesdell.

Dick looked at Utley, and both men laughed. "Give us your roster, Craig," said Dick.

Utley made a businesslike report. As did Dick. He wanted to get home.

Truesdell was adding check marks alongside the names on a legal-length tablet he had. "I hope I passed?" Utley asked politely as he concluded. He had only five students and his report was routine when compared to Dick's knowledge of his six.

"I may go into personalities on my final report," Dick warned Truesdell. "At this point, I don't feel prepared to do so. I have one black. I have one woman student. Each feels the *onus* of that circumstance."

"Why should you make it an *onus?*" asked Truesdell.

"Oh, come on, now, Doctor!" cried Utley. "It damn well would make a difference if you had those two types!"

"I doubt it," said Truesdell.

Truesdell made a point of looking at his watch. "Get on with your report, Foster."

"Yes, sir. Oh, yes, *sir!* All right. I have six students. One is invariably late, but that can be cured. I've had a few problems with the black student, though generally of a personal nature. He wants to hurry up, become a doctor, and make money. He suggests shortcuts, and sees no need for the sheets to be changed during his two weeks."

"Dr. Foster . . ."

"All right, all right. I had Jackson observe some very skillful and difficult abdominal surgery and he fell asleep. He is inclined to argue on both medical and personal points. He is poor, and he resents people who are not poor.

"The other minority student I have, the young woman, Alice Baus, works too hard, and makes me work too hard. She'll make it in med school. I've already reported her attendance and grade record. But I am not so sure Baus will do as well living with us as Jackson has done, sheets or no."

"Why not?"

"Because she is a woman. My wife may

not — Well, all this will be in the next report. Alice is hard-working, she does well. I like the ones I can count on to be clean and well-behaved."

"Aren't they all?"

"Now you know damn well they are not. I think I have one lad who knows about drugs. I have a very serious student who is about to skip a year of college work by taking exams."

"He's rich."

"His family seems to be. But he is quite serious about studying medicine. He and Jackson don't get along, of course. Jackson's fault."

"This Jackson —"

"I'd like to see him make it," said Dick, "in spite of himself."

"It takes up your time."

Dick gathered his papers together. "It all takes time, Truesdell."

"I believe we should weed out these problems before they get into med school."

Dick said nothing; Utley followed him from the room. Dick was thinking that, at the beginning of the meeting — and they had not waited for Truesdell to make his detailed report — the so-called leader had classified his students as run-of-the-mill medical students. One eager-beaver, two goof-offs, one dumb, one smart.

Dick had the same; how he treated them might make the difference.

Utley caught at his arm. "What do you make of Truesdell?" he asked.

"I think he is getting paid for leading this program."

"If you find he is —"

"I'd still do it on my own. But I'd get him out. And I learned just this week that we get the students from low-income families through a Metropolitan Talent Search program funded by a fifty-thousand-dollar grant. Somebody is getting that money."

"Not me."

"Nor me. But I'm about to find out about Truesdell."

"D'you think he is out to subvert this program?"

"He could be. I know the students compare notes on us. And I suspect that at least one of mine reports to Truesdell."

"How did he get steered that way?"

"Jan asked him if he did. At the time he said he didn't, but I believe she gave him the idea, which he may have followed up."

"Damn it, Foster, we are putting in too much time —"

"I know that, and I resent it. Right now, my problem is going to be to get to know Baus. The female. Really know her. Somebody is going to put a stick in that wheel, I'll bet."

Utley looked troubled. "I'll help you if you need it."

"I'll probably call on you. Do you — of course you do! I mean while you and I went through our schooling without subsidies and all this, I still am young enough to realize that the students we docents are getting are just about the same as we were, and our classmates. We did the same things, we caught up on our sleep and evaded a task, using the same ploys. Even the nicknames. Big Doc. Old Doc."

Utley laughed. "And you have *Ms.* Baus."

"Not if I can help it. I hate the term. Along with chairpersons and committee creatures."

"Where did you read or hear that one?"

"I quickly forgot that, too."

Utley laughed and they parted, Dick to return to his office and a joint meeting of his docent students. Should he tell them, as he meant to tell Kenneth, that Truesdell thought they were going to run into trouble? He decided that he would avoid quoting Truesdell, but he did tell Kenneth, and he went on to tell his students to seize every opportunity they were given to learn, that they were never to think that he and Dr. Harrington were the only doctors to teach or to emulate.

"We far from know all there is to know," he said. He pointed to a stack of books and thin pamphlets on his desk. "Just now I am working harder than you do, to gain an understanding of multiple sclerosis."

"Do you treat that, Doctor?" asked the student Reed Crans.

"No, but I often have to diagnose it. Oh, not *often,* thank God. Though once a year is often enough. That's what a primary doctor does. He learns to know and spot the symptoms, then hands the case on to the neurologist."

"And that one tells you if you're wrong," said Jackson.

"Yes, he does," Dick agreed calmly. Jackson had yet to get under his skin.

"Do you have such a case?" asked Alice Baus. "Now, I mean."

"I did have, a month or so ago. In this case, the woman died within two weeks, and because it was so acute a case, an autopsy was done. I suggested that special attention should be paid to the brain. We know that sclerosis destroys the myelin, or protecting covering of important nerve fibers. And in this case there were areas of inflammation, and on the edges of the lesions there was evidence of attack on the myelin by antibody and local scavenger cells called macrophages." He paused to spell the word. "So now we feel sure that adult sclerosis is caused, or at least involves auto-immune processes or unusual virus infections, perhaps both."

He paused and rubbed his hand down his face. "I'm sorry," he said. "I forgot you are not even medical students."

"You make a good teacher," said Crans.

Dick flushed. "There will be changes the end of this week," he said. "Mrs. Baus will spend two intensive weeks with me or Dr. Harrington. The rest of you meet as notified. Are there any questions?"

Jackson stood up. "Do I go back to your house now?"

"I will stop at Research to make rounds. Then, yes, we go home."

"And play with the dolls," drawled the tall man. Every student looked up in protest. Dr. Foster was a very successful physician, they all had learned that. He was well liked, and had risen fast. His treatment of them deserved respect.

Now he stood gazing at Jackson. "A doctor's life," he said slowly, "is a short one. He doesn't really start his own work until he is twenty-eight or thirty. By the time he is sixty, sometimes sooner, his sharpness has departed. Many doctors feel obliged to retire then. If he has other interests, hobbies he enjoys, that retirement is more pleasant for him and his friends. My hobby happens to be — well, no matter if you call it playing with dolls. Try it and see if you can do it. I am going over to Research. Good evening, gentlemen."

Gathering up his medical bag and his briefcase, he left the room, hearing the babble of voices behind him.

"What stirred him up?" Kenny asked Leslie.

"Jackson probably. That fellow is insufferable. Here comes the rest of the gang."

It was Kenneth who reminded Jackson that he was supposed to accompany Dr. Foster.

"I'll catch up," said Jackson. "There ain't no hurry."

"If you have extra time," said Kenneth stiffly, "you might give some thought to your grammar. You are not going to survive med school or get an internship speaking as you do."

"I plan to work among my friends," said Jackson, swaggering off.

"How does Dick make his reports on Jackson?" Kenny asked Leslie.

"Performance adequate," she said. "But I think there are things about Jackson that concern Dick more than his grammar. That's deliberate, you know."

"And I let him score," groaned Kenny. "Well, good night, sweetheart. I think the last of the docents have left. You can lock up. See you tomorrow."

"I always do."

"Dull, isn't it?"

"Not very, Doctor. Not very."

Dick went to Research, he made his rounds, and Jackson caught up with him as he checked the roster at Sister Alphonsus' desk. "You can wait in the car," Dick said to him shortly.

The Administrator watched the tall man go down the hall. "Did you give him permission to come over here on his own?" she asked.

Dick looked up, frowning. "Why should he do that?"

"And go up to the top floors?"

"Certainly not!"

"I understand he has been up there."

"I'll speak to him."

"What did he do to make you mad today?" she asked keenly.

Dick laughed. "Nothing, really. I suppose my working with miniatures does seem like child's play to some men."

"It should not!" said Sister indignantly. "You have the skill of a surgeon! You do beautiful work."

Dick looked at his hands. "Do you think I should be doing surgery?" he asked.

"I think you are doing fine work in your own field. And I have something for you." She handed him a rolled magazine. "Read it when you get through this evening, if you ever do. Good night, Doctor. Rest well."

Dick thanked her and went out. He found Jackson under the wheel of his car. "I'll drive, Doctor, then you can rest and recuperate."

Dick stood waiting. And Jackson slid over. "I'll find me something to recuperate from," he said.

"You do that. And after this, do not go up to the top floors of Research."

"Why should I . . . ?"

"Just don't do it," said Dick. "Again."

"Whut we goin' to do at home?"

"Pray that we don't get called out. If we don't, I'll let you help me enlarge the south rose bed."

"And ruin my hands?" asked Jackson in dismay.

"Better yours than mine. I've already made my M.D."

"You threatenin' me, Doctor?"

"Just commenting."

"I'd rather help you play with your doll furniture."

"I know you would."

They drove home; there were no calls. Dick changed clothes and gave Jackson a shovel. He worked right along with him.

Gene strolled over and asked the student what part of medicine he was learning.

"How to retire, Mr. Foster. That's the best reason I can think of."

Even Dick laughed. They went in for dinner. Which was good. Dick told Jackson he could study, watch TV, or go to bed. "I don't need you in my doll house," he said. And he disappeared into the basement workshop where Gene again joined him. "What's wrong?" he asked.

"Oh, a lot of niggling things came up today. Gene, does anyone ever come down here when I am away?"

"You lock the outside door."

"I know."

"Is something missing?"

"Yes. I was making two mirror frames. You know — oval — beaded and painted with gold paint."

"Sure I know. They are pretty."

"I think so. But I could swear I had made

two ready for painting. Last session I cut the glass."

"Yes, you did, and I told you that if I were doing it, I'd cut the glass first, and make the frames to fit it."

"Yes, you did tell me that. But —" He pushed forward a single oval. "I can't find the second mirror."

They looked. It was not there. Dick decided that he would have to make a second one.

"I'd say to hell with it, and make only one."

"Not if you were making doll houses for twins I know."

The twins would be Gene's nieces, and he smiled at his brother. "Have you seen this week's issue of *Personalities*?" he asked.

"I haven't seen last week's." Dick was all concentration on cutting the curve of wood.

"Well, you would be interested in this one. Because they've done a profile on a local young doctor, very successful, popular with everyone. He has risen fast and high. There are pictures of his home. Looks just exactly like my next-door neighbor's."

Dick laid down his sharp chisel.

"They tell about his hobbies, his roses, his skill with miniature furniture done exactly to scale. Mentions your trips to art museums and homes on display to get things correct and in scale."

"My trips," murmured Dick.

"Didn't they interview you?"

"They may have. Gee whiz, Gene . . ."

"You really should read it. You'd admire this young fella."

Sister Alphonsus had given him a magazine. Dick picked up the chisel.

But Gene was relentless. "It tells that you are a docent . . ."

"And explains what that means?"

"It tries."

"That's good. I seem to be keeping strange company lately."

"Yeah, and the article quotes what some of that company has to say about you."

Dick turned to look sharply at his brother. "Which ones?" he demanded.

"You can read the whole thing. I have the magazine."

"Sister gave me one at Research."

"And you ignored it."

"I wanted to get that rose bed out of Jackson. Did he testify on me as a docent?"

"No, he evidently was not asked. There was a girl —"

"Yes. Alice Baus. She starts two weeks with me on Monday."

"She thinks you are working at less than your capabilities."

Dick chuckled. "A lot she knows."

"And a sharp-sounding man who said you should be appreciated."

"Reed Crans?"

"Yes."

"He's older. He has his college degree. I have my eye on him to come into our office ten years from now. He probably doesn't work for money."

"You do all right."

"By working my tail off. Who else gave out?"

"Staff doctors, patients. The women just love you."

"Yeah, yeah."

"The author says he couldn't get a good interview with you, that you were too busy to give him the time, but in the same paragraph he mentioned that you had a relaxed air, pretty blue eyes, and a patient manner under stress."

Dick laughed. "I don't believe a word you are saying."

"Read it, son. Read it. Tells all about your pretty home, says you have no children, and that your wife is the former Janice Bryant."

Dick made a sound of protest, and bent over the workbench.

"Okay," said Gene. "I won't say more."

"You will, but I always forgive you. Be

careful crossing through the grass, big brother. I stubbed my toe on a sprinkler head in broad daylight."

"I'm the graceful one of the family." And Gene departed.

Dick regarded the small progress he had made on the mirror frame and decided he would quit and go upstairs. Janice would be angry if she had read the article. But then she had been angry ever since the meeting and the development of the docent program.

He locked away his tools. He went upstairs and washed his hands and forearms, looked down at his shoes. He had put on sneakers before eating dinner.

And then he went to join his wife and Jackson, who were watching TV. He stopped in the kitchen for a glass of milk, drank it, and went into the adjoining family room. He thought that Gene's quoted article was right. He did have a fine home, and Jan kept it exquisitely. The kitchen was gleaming white with shelf edges and door trim in delft blue. The family room was essentially the same shade of blue — bookshelves, benches and table, the cushions on the couch —

Jackson made a perfunctory move to relinquish his place to Dick, who shook his head and sat down in the armchair.

Jan rose and took a magazine from the table and shoved it toward Dick. "Though I am aware you have read it," she said.

Dick was right. She was angry about the article. Cold angry. He laid the magazine aside.

"Gene told me about it," he said quietly.

"Did you go over there? I thought —"

"He came downstairs. We talked about an item that seems to have disappeared from my workbench, and he told me the high spots of the article. Sister also gave me a copy. It's out in the car."

"I'd hardly think you would need publicity," said Jan. "And a write-up like that strikes me as unethical as paid-for advertising."

Dick said nothing. He leaned his head back and closed his eyes. Jan was trying to needle him into a response in front of Jackson. She would not make it.

"There's an interesting article in tonight's paper, too," Jan persisted. "If we ever get the medical school you want, Dick, you might have the same experience. It tells about a medical school official who has been stealing through a scheme involving ghost employees."

Dick controlled his muscles, but his attention focused. Sister had said the Surgical business office —

". . . she," Jan persisted, "admitted helping two relatives receive forty thousand dollars from the school though she herself did not get a penny."

"I wouldn't buy that," said Jackson.

Neither would Dick.

"Well, she admitted hiring a man and a woman — it gives their names — and signed payroll authorization though neither of the two worked for the school."

"How long did that go on?" Dick asked.

"Five years, until the woman was fired from her job. But I'm like Jackson. I don't believe she did not get a payoff."

"The court isn't buying it either," said Dick. "It seems they found canceled checks written to her by the so-called employees."

"You know about it?" Jan asked in surprise.

"Yes. Sister thinks, or thought, she might have a couple of ghosts there."

"Does she?"

"Not that we can identify. In fact, I think I met one of the ghosts the other day."

Jackson laughed. Jan stared at her husband. "I didn't tell you this as a joke," she said stiffly.

"I know you didn't. But ghosts often turn

up in hospitals and medical schools. I thought I saw one some time ago on the top floor of Research."

Jackson stirred uneasily. "I think I'll go upstairs and study," he said.

"Don't overdo," drawled Dick, picking up the magazine which Jan had given him. The pictures accompanying the article were excellent.

He became aware that Jackson had stopped before his chair. "Now what?" he said, looking up.

"I been thinkin' about that girl we had in the office this afternoon," said the black man. "She ain't bright, is she?"

"Maggie is retarded, yes."

"An' she's pregnant?"

"I'm afraid so, Jackson. But —"

"I know you don't like me to talk about cases and things here at the house in front of your wife, and all."

"Then why do it? I need a rest and change from the office," said Dick. "And some cases are complicated. It would take too long to explain the whole picture which we have in the files. I am a family doctor, and our hope is that we docents can train some of our medical students to be family doctors. The community needs them."

"Yes, sir, I can see that."

"After the end of this week, you are to report at the clinics downtown. You will be given a schedule."

He looked down again at the magazine.

"Doc . . ." said Jackson uneasily. Jan was pretending to work on some needlepoint, but Dick knew that she was listening keenly.

"Could it wait?" Dick asked.

"I just wanted to ask, isn't that Maggie Hart chile awful young?"

"Fourteen. Yes, that is young. But these days, chicks get wise early. In this case, Maggie, being retarded, had no idea of what she was doing. She and a friendly neighbor boy play ball together, and evidently they had other amusements. I asked her who the father was, and had to be very explicit before she could answer me."

"Are you going to do a 'bortion?"

"I don't do abortions, Jackson, and I don't order them except in extreme cases."

"And you don't think this is extreme?" asked Jan. "A retarded girl of fourteen? What becomes of her child? Won't it also be retarded? Or handicapped in some way?"

Dick slapped the magazine back on the table. "Now you two listen to me," he said. "And I am giving you an order, Jackson. I do not talk about office cases out in public or in my home. This is a prime example of why I do not. We have this sad accident come into the office. I know the family — because I am a family doctor. There is no reason to think that Maggie's baby will be retarded. However, we shall make tests."

"But she —"

"Her retardation is due to a birth injury," said Dick, biting off the words. "There is no reason why she should not have a normal child. Her parents are heartsick about this. They were trying to find ways to protect Maggie, who has a mental age of five, without making her afraid to play with other children. She has no idea of what is happening to her.

"Now we shall take care of her, and the parents will raise the child as if it were their own. And" — he turned to leave — "don't let anything be said about the situation as unfortunately it has been discussed here tonight. In other words, both of you, button your lips!"

He walked out of the room. Jackson might obey, for fear of being denied entrance into medical school. Jan would surely talk about it in her various club circles. And he would be left with even more problems than he had brought home from the office. Ghosts, indeed! He could handle them. It was the live and bodied people who made trouble.

* * *

The next day he told Kenneth Harrington what had happened. "Someone stole one of my pretties, and Jackson flapped his lips in front of Jan about the Maggie Hart case. I think you can take on Alice Baus next week. I'll go somewhere for a rest cure."

"What do you suppose Jackson is going after?"

"I think sometimes that Jan puts him in line. And we know what she wants."

"Then there should be no more live-in students."

"It's Truesdell's program that we give them each two weeks in our homes."

Kenny's opinion of Truesdell was unprintable.

Dick mentioned his very faint suspicion that Jackson had been exploring Research Hospital, even its empty upper floors. Why, he asked, would he do that?

"Find out what he wants, and you'll know."

"Did he steal the little mirror? Did he tell Jan about Maggie Hart's baby? She'd been briefed on that."

"She's active in the LIFE movement. If she thought you would order an abortion —"

"Well, she misjudged me."

"Can't I take Jackson for the last couple of days?"

"We'd have to explain. He — and Jan — would think our reason was Maggie's case."

"Let them. You've shown your displeasure."

"That should end the matter, shouldn't it?"

"Not if he is getting ready to blackmail you."

"Bonkers!"

"No, it isn't. Remember there are other places who would publish an article about you. One that would not mention your pretty blue eyes. I can think of a dozen lines another writer could take."

Dick made some notes on his appointment calendar. "Have you seen Maria Pollack this morning?"

"Yes, Doctor," said Kenny, watching him.

Dick threw his pencil across the desk. "All right. Let's have it. I did make the fella dig a rose bed last night."

Kenny laughed. "Insult to injury."

"He took it that way. I'll wash down his bed when he leaves."

"I think you'd better. As for the other ways and means. Where are you sleeping these nights?"

Dick flushed. "Jan thinks I get more rest in my own room."

"I've heard her say that. Do you?"

"Do I what? Get more rest?"

"Do you?"

"I do all right."

"All right isn't good enough, is it?"

"Hey, what is all this? Who's blackmailing now?"

"I'm just showing you where the path leads. Is it good enough?"

No, it was not. But Dick would not say so. And did not.

"Paying blackmail is always a mistake, Doctor."

"In theory, yes, it is."

"What does she want?"

So it was "she" now. "You know the small-town, farm bit."

"Yes, I know it. But if she's stepped up her pressure . . ."

Through Jackson. Yes, she could have.

Dick's forearms prickled. Leslie! If Jackson had said one word about Leslie . . .

The beautifully illustrated magazine would attract attention. To follow it with a smutty story involving . . . Yes! There could be blackmail. "I don't believe this docent program was properly worked out," he said stiffly, and went into his office, closing the door firmly behind him.

Kenneth stood for a minute staring at the door, marked only with a narrow name label of silver on black. *Dr. Foster.* Which was what Dick was. What he wanted to be.

It made a man damn mad, he told Leslie when he went out to the office to get the morning's hospital calls. Dick was staying in.

Leslie's list for him would keep him busy. "What's bothering you?" she asked coolly.

"I'm red-hot mad, but I thought I wouldn't show it."

"With that round and honest face of yours," said Leslie, "you can't conceal a thing. What's happened to you?"

"To Dick." He rested his bag on the edge of her desk. "Now, I argue that a man of his caliber — Have you seen the *Personality* article?"

"Yes. Great. Simply great!"

"It was, but it can make trouble for Dick."

Leslie frowned. "The telephone . . ."

"I know. More patients. And still more. But —" And he spilled the whole thing out, speaking rapidly, softly. Already there were four patients waiting.

As he talked, Leslie's face went pale under her carefully unnoticeable makeup.

"I think we had better not talk about it," she said softly when Kenny had finished. "That much is about all we can do."

"You're right. I'll be where you say I'll be," he told her, smiling at her over his shoulder as he went down the hall to the door and the parking lot.

He was where he was supposed to be. All

morning, he worked. First he went over to Research, and agreed with Sister in her opinion of the article about Dick Foster. "I think they should have made a little more over his wife," she said.

"Do you know Jan?"

"No, I don't. Just by sight. She isn't friendly the way the doctor is."

On that, Kenny made no comment. He went up to see Maria Pollack, and then looked in on three other patients they had at Research. He read charts, asked to see some X rays, and wrote orders. One man, a stroke patient, said he'd wait until Dr. Foster had time to see him."

Kenny was used to that. This patient gave even Dick trouble.

"I'm off to Children's," he told Sister when he went through the lobby. "I'll stop at the clinic on my way."

"They've got measles down there. At Children's."

Kenny stopped short. "How . . . ?"

Sister shrugged. "Some children don't get the shots, and when one gets measles, the others do, too."

Besides the pregnant mothers. "Rubella?" he asked. "I hope not."

Sister shrugged. "I'm afraid that's what it is."

Kenny whistled and went out. Should he talk to Dick about this? No. Dick had a very full schedule, besides the decision on what and how to do about the Hart girl. "You're a big boy, Kenneth," he said under his breath as he started the car.

But rubella in one of the city's free clinics . . . He whistled softly. The problem was to get these people to keep their immunization records. To them, a card from the doctor was only a card, and they soon forgot what "shots" their children had had and when.

And these children were bussed back and forth about the town to schools; their mothers worked in homes. It was not at all difficult to set up a small infection.

There was another clinic, farther downtown, called the Medical Center. This one was "the clinic," and it was staffed by a former paramedic and a practical nurse, with a clerk to keep records and answer the telephone. The doctors of the city did attending duty, rotating their services. Kenny was obligated for two hours there that morning. He talked a lot about the measles thing, and had warnings put up for the other doctors as well as such patients as could and would read them.

He always enjoyed Children's Hospital, but there too he posted the measles warnings. He called in to the office to say he would eat lunch at Children's, then go on to General. "Tell Dick they have a couple of measles cases at the clinic."

"He'll be happy to hear. When can you get back here?"

"Am I needed?"

"Wanted, dear. Wanted."

"Then I'll hustle. How does two sound?"

"Not as if you'd make it, but try."

Kenny went to the staff dining room for lunch and talked to his friends there about the measles situation. No, there were not many cases, but even one —

The lunch was simple, and good. Bowls of tomato soup, platters of good sausages, rye and white bread for sandwiches, and a great wooden bowl of tossed salad. A plate of cookies beside the coffee urn on a side table.

The men asked about Dick, and mentioned the article in the magazine. It was so good, said one, that Foster would be getting offers for a TV series. The pictures were exceptionally good. Did he really weave the tiny bedspreads and draperies?

"Yes, he has a small hand loom which he made. He does all the work on the furniture, buying the appropriate woods. He really gets absorbed, which is what he needs."

"Does his wife . . . ?" asked a new, young

doctor, and fell silent, puzzled at the laughter which went hooting around the table. He had met Dr. Foster, he said lamely.

There were several of the doctors ready to explain the situation in the Foster home. "It's just a matter of the wrong woman married to the right man," said the only female doctor at the table.

"A rather trite situation," agreed an older man, "of a wife who can't or won't keep up with her husband's success."

"There are variations on that trite story," said another man, who was wearing surgical greens and kept his eye on the clock.

Finally someone asked Kenny what he knew; he worked with Dick Foster.

Kenny hesitated. "We don't talk too much about that subject," he said. "I know very little beyond the fact that they were married when Dick was an intern. Jan herself has no degree."

"She can always get one, from the University here, or one nearby."

"They have no children," someone explained to the newcomer.

"She could go to a charm school," said another man sourly. "She looks and acts like a Buddha."

There was both laughter and protest to that.

"The best thing she could do for herself as well as Dick would be to give him children. He would really like that."

"Can't she, or won't she?" Everyone looked at Kenny.

He shrugged. "We have never discussed the point. I think — No, I think I'll shut up and go on to General."

He knew that he left talk and surmise behind him.

Chapter 3

Time had a way of going along on greased wheels. Though it really was not too long after the talk with Gene that Dick found himself, almost without warning, asking Jan what it was she wanted out of their life together. "Well," he amended, "what was it you wanted when you married me?"

She considered this a surprising question. She rested her chin on the heel of her hand, which in turn was supported by the elbow which rested on the small table where she sat.

"What are you doing, anyway?" Dick asked her. "Just now, I mean."

She looked down at the litter of newspapers, scissors, and paper clips. "Cutting coupons," she told him, as if her explanation was much more reasonable than his question.

"Coupons for what?" he asked.

"Oh, all sorts of things." She picked up a small stack of paper of various sizes and colors. "Camera film, coffee, a new soap —"

Dick had seen such coupons. "Do you

cash them?" he asked.

"Some of them. The others I give to Marlene; she has such a huge family —"

Almost constantly, some of that family were visiting at Gene's. Dick enjoyed the young people, and envied his brother. His own house was always as neat as a pin, and as silent as a church on Monday morning.

"I wish what you wanted was a family," he told his wife. "Our marriage would have some meaning then."

"Are you talking about divorce?" Jan demanded, dropping a mutilated sheet of newspaper into the wastebasket at her side.

"I'd hope not."

"You sound that way."

Dick felt his nerves tighten. "I simply asked you what you wanted out of our marriage. Perhaps divorce is in your mind."

"It isn't. I keep a good house for you. I try to do things as you like them."

Yes. Breakfast was always ready and hot in the morning, dinner at night unless he was delayed. Shining floors, a pleasing arrangement of furniture, colors, fabrics . . .

"Sometime," he said, "I'll copy this house and display it. I bet I'd win a prize."

She was complimented, and showed her pleasure. "I like to keep house," she admitted.

"Even with my docents underfoot?"

"Well, Jackson and I got along —"

"You were the only one who did. Do you know? He asked Sister Alphonsus if he could live in one of the empty rooms at Research. He said it would save his having to find a cheap room in town."

"But Sister Alphonsus wouldn't let him."

"Not Jackson."

"He wasn't so bad."

"He was, and is, bad. He'll never make it through med school."

"Why not?"

"He takes every shortcut possible. And you can't do that in medicine. Not even studying it as they do today — active participation over and above the book part."

"Will our late-departed Mrs. Baus make it?"

"I think so."

"I wouldn't want her for a doctor."

Dick considered that. "I suppose I wouldn't pick her out as my own physician," he decided. "But given the choice, God forbid, I'd take her over Jackson every time."

"Is Kenny taking the next one?"

"He wants to. He took Alice Baus for a week, remember. But the 'next one' won't be until next month. They are having spring break at school."

"Doctors don't get spring breaks."

"As a matter of fact, most of them do. There's an internist I know pretty well who takes his whole family to a horse ranch every September, and after New Year's, he always plays golf at Hilton Island."

"He must be doing well."

"He is. Charges fearful consultant fees."

"You could do the same."

"Is that what you want me to do?"

She cut out another coupon. "We don't have a whole family to take to Colorado, and you don't play golf."

"Well, then we're back where we started. What comes next for us?"

She spoke thoughtfully. "Not the divorce you suggested."

"It was you who . . ."

She hushed him with a raised hand. He wished she would cut those damn bangs, or brush them smoothly together on her forehead. He started to list what he had heard Jan say so many times before.

"Let me make the answer," he said. "I've heard it so often that I know it by heart. You don't like to live in the city, or even as far out as we do. My practice is in the city, and you would like me to abandon it and move — go — to a small town. Say, fifteen thousand people.

"We could buy a farm, a small one, which

you would run. We'd raise goats that stink like hell, and sunflowers for the seed, and sorghum cane. You would have the perfect vegetable garden."

"I would, Dick."

"Oh, I don't doubt for a minute that you would. And raise in it all the vegetables that I despise. Eggplant, brussels sprouts, parsnips . . ."

"Some people —"

"Yes, some people do like those things. I don't happen to. I would have to learn to like them, I suppose, just as I would have to learn to live and practice in a small town although I have lived in a city all my life, and done my work here."

"I know that," said Jan calmly, "but you say all the time that big medicine is changing —"

"I say that it is changing all the time. I don't often speak of professional matters here at home."

"No, you don't, but you might if we lived where I'd know your patients and could help them in my own way."

"I believe you are still thinking about divorce. You'd be much happier married to a small-town guy who would gossip with you and his patients." As he never would do, and she knew it.

For ten minutes she snip-snipped at her coupons, and he read an editorial in the newspaper. He agreed with it so he read it again.

"What do you mean," Jan asked unexpectedly, "when you say big medicine is changing so rapidly?"

Her question surprised him, but he decided that he could answer her seriously. "Well, there's equipment, of course. And people who must know how to use it. Computers. And then there are the emergency rooms."

Her head went up.

"That's right," Dick told her. "Every hospital has to enlarge its facilities because people come to them for every and any reason. Outpatient types turn the things into general practice offices. They used to be staffed by residents and interns working in rotation. Now they have specialists, doctors good at diagnosis, able to judge a condition quickly and accurately. The E.R. is probably the prototype of the governmental medical unit of the future. And discoveries like the structure of the immune bodies open up a whole new ball game in medicine. If I'm still around thirty years from now, I'll see very different medicine from what I practice and teach today."

"Better?"

"Maybe. Like us, the doctors of today, the

doctors of thirty years from now will do the best they can."

"Hmmmmn. Thirty years. You'd be just a bit over sixty-five. And you'd have to work to keep up."

"Yes, of course."

"But you'd not need to stay with it and be upset. A small-town doctor doesn't have big, complicated machines, and things like immune bodies."

Dick laughed. He reached for a pad of paper and took out his pencil, began to sketch. "I never did find that little mirror I think Jackson stole."

"Wait a minute. I want to say some more —"

"There's nothing more to say, Jan. I'd read and attend convocations even if I were a small-town doctor. And I can't think that being upset in the country would be any improvement on my being upset in my present offices. The pregnant retarded girl would still bring the problem of abortion right up to my desk."

"I don't believe, usually, in abortion."

"Neither do I, normally. But here, with other men around me, working, studying, I can go along with a movement and put on the brakes where and when I think they are needed."

"You would make a good country doctor."

"I make a good city one. Surely the city folk should have one compassionate man in their service."

She often mentioned this hope of hers, but that spring and summer she persisted with it. During Mrs. Baus' two weeks with Dick she had talked about it. She and Alice Baus tolerated each other. The young woman asked to use the washing machine, and she kept her room neat. This satisfied Jan. But Alice was not a talker. As Jackson had been. Though Jan must have suspected that she listened, even when she appeared to be reading or studying, because she made a rather awkward effort to include her in one of her active discussions of her ideas of where the Doctor should be practicing. They were eating dinner, and Dick watched the two women with interest. A generation apart in age, he thought they might have interests in common. If Jan had ever been at all interested in his profession, she would have been the same intense, pushy type of student as was Alice Baus.

He ate his chicken and his lettuce, and listened to Jan describe the farm community which, according to her, needed Dick's presence.

"Do you know this area?" the student asked the doctor.

"Not as well as Mrs. Foster. It's where she was born and grew up. I suspect there have been changes."

"But they need doctors," said Jan intensely. "You know they do."

"They need them, yes." He thought of the life which Jan would live while he occupied the office he could have in such a place, and attended such patients as would come to him. Home calls, minor illnesses — and a trip to the city to see a specialist if and when something serious developed. He, as a doctor, would send them to the specialists. He could lose his "experience"; he could not afford the needed equipment. He thought of the man who, that day, had come gasping and weak to their office. He needed pneumo-therapy immediately, and he got it, then was transferred to Research, where Dick or Kenny would watch him.

Though the rural people did need doctors. Two-days-a-week clinics seemed to be working —

Jan would enjoy living on a farm again, a member of the active little church, busy with bake sales, homecomings, centennial celebrations.

"Are you planning to move to the country?"

Mrs. Baus was asking him.

Dick picked up his coffee cup. "No, I don't think so. I seem to be filling a need here. We might get some acreage out into the country where Mrs. Foster could raise vegetables, but as things are now, I couldn't consider a move."

"I've asked you to consider it," said Jan, thinly. And she had, and probably would exert pressure. Kenny called it blackmail. He would not mention that here and now.

"I have thought about it," he said quietly. "And I'll continue to think about it."

As Jan served dessert, he thought, smiling, about the second "ghost" on the surgery office payroll whom he had encountered that day. He must find time to talk to Sister and get that mystery cleared up. Why and how had the word got about that there were ghosts?

He barely tasted his pie. "Mrs. Baus and I are going out," he told Jan. "Save that. I may be hungry when I get home."

Alice Baus looked at him in surprise. "Where are you going?"

"To talk to the family of that woman who can't decide about having a hip replacement."

Jan made a grimace of revulsion.

"If you had such a painful arthritic hip," Dick said quietly, "the idea would open the doors of paradise to you."

"If I had an arthritic hip, I'd go to bed and stay there."

She would not, but Dick did not argue the point. He told Mrs. Baus to be ready in fifteen minutes. "I'll go over and check on my brother, and wait in the car. Thank you for a good dinner, Jan," he said as he went toward the side door.

On the drive to the patient's home, he discussed with his pupil the replacement of a hip joint. Was it safe? With a capable surgeon of course it was safe. Effective? There again, various elements must be considered. The surgeon's skill, the nature of the patient, her physical makeup. Bones, blood, a dozen items entered the thing.

"And the support of the family."

Smart girl. "Yes, that is essential."

"Wouldn't any family . . . ?"

"No. A lot of families would support Jan's stated procedure. Bed, and death. This woman — her painful hip condition has grown worse during the past year. Total replacement seems to me to be the only hope for her, and I want to convince her family. It is, I think, one of the great advancements made in the treatment of arthritis."

"Is it always successful?"

Dick sat smiling. *"Always,"* he said, "is a

word we doctors don't use much. But it often is successful, and makes the patient much more comfortable and more able to get around. Of course it is a major operation, and is usually done only on patients with a severe crippling disability. There is some risk, but not a great one."

"As her doctor, you decide?"

"With the help of an orthopedic surgeon, yes, we can best evaluate the patient's condition and recommend what is really going to help."

"Shouldn't you be a surgeon?"

"If I were, some primary doctor would have to bring this patient to my attention."

They had reached their destination, a large apartment house. "If you operate, can I watch?" asked the student.

"Certainly. Just keep reminding me. Let's go in —" She had not asked him to describe the surgery. Probably she had read up on that. She was going to make a good doctor. Worth the time he was giving her.

The same was true of Reed Crans. He was the student who excited Dick, and he realized that he must be showing it. Jan's instant dislike of him confirmed his suspicion. She had enjoyed Jackson, she tolerated Baus, but when Crans moved in —

"He's as old as you are!" declared Jan.

"He is twenty-three. And that's a long way back for me."

"Why . . . ?"

"He plans to study medicine. That's all I need to know."

"And me, too?"

He did not reply. It was not the way he wished things could be with Jan, but silence often was his only protection. He had come to be glad that he was so busy that he had little time to worry about his domestic situation. One of these days —

Meanwhile he enjoyed Crans. The man was older. He had already taken a degree in Business. He could quickly take the necessary courses to give him his BS in pre-medicine. He was well-mannered and pleasant. A dark-skinned fellow with a puckish grin, he talked intelligently to Dick about the profession of medicine. He surely could be no trouble to Jan, no more than the extra plate on the dinner table. He was courteous to her always.

He was fascinated with the miniaturizing carpentry which Dick did. Wasn't there a field in medicine where instruments . . . ?

"Yes," Dick agreed eagerly. "At times I've worked with the fella at General who makes corrective braces and special instruments for the doctors. It's a big help to the pediatricians —"

Crans showed active interest in the work done in Dick's offices, and asked about the retarded girl who was pregnant.

"Do you docent students talk about the cases to each other?" Dick asked. Jackson had been "in" on that sad case.

"Yes, we do. And about the doctors, too."

"Oh, no!" laughed Dick. "Need I caution you about talk to outsiders?"

"Not me," said Reed Crans. "I can't speak for the others."

"No." Dr. Truesdell would lecture them if it were necessary. "Now, about that unfortunate girl. She will go to work in the Salvation Army Home until her baby is born. They are very kind and understanding people. If her family rejects the child, it can be put up for adoption."

"You have decisions all the time?"

"What business is your father in?"

"He has a brokerage company. My older brother has gone in with him on that. But they asked me, and I am venturing to repeat the question to you. You can answer or not. But one hears about the great riches doctors earn . . . Incidentally that is not my reason —"

Dick put up his hand. "I understand that."

As they talked, Dick thought of the three

students who had been in his home. Jackson, inquisitive, gossipy, and sly. He probably would stay with the medicine project, and make a good living from it.

Which had been the question under discussion with Crans that evening. His parents had discussed the subject, no doubt wanting him to stay with the family business.

"Can't they afford a doctor in the family?" Dick had asked, waiting for a traffic light.

"They would rather know how far I can go to afford to be one."

"I can't give you a definite answer, Reed. I read recently in the newspaper that a busy doctor makes a hundred thousand a year."

Reed Crans whistled.

"That sometimes involves skill in medicine, sometimes bedside manner, sometimes finagling. I suspect a few doctors use all three."

"I see the first two in your office."

"I am considered successful, but one has to consider the pie."

Reed had turned his head to look at him.

"Sure," said Dick. "Incidentally, it is the pie which my wife feels could be dropped from my work. But I haven't dropped it, so this is the way the experts say it goes, and I suspect they are right. Based on our hypothetical hundred thousand — the pie — we slice it as Jan sliced her lemon pie tonight. I don't have the figures exact; you or your father could get them, but the slices go something like this. The pie is the doctor's dollar, assuming that he earns it and collects it. One cent goes for depreciation of medical equipment —"

"Broken test tubes, a typewriter needing repair —"

"That's it. We'll use my office as an example, though doctors make more money in fields like surgery. Dr. Utley is a urologist, and he does. Anyway, we'll work on my dollar. A penny for depreciation, two pennies for professional car upkeep —" His hand slapped the wheel of his "professional" car. "Then there is a three-cent slice to pay for drugs and medical supplies. Alcohol to swab an arm before a shot. All the things needed and used in a doctor's office. Swabs, Kleenex — underpads for the examination tables —

"An equal sum pays for malpractice insurance."

Reed looked at him in surprise. "I would have said it would be larger."

"That's large enough. Our slices are getting into the body of the pie. The next one takes five cents. For office space. Either a doctor owns or rents such space. I rent. Then there's a large sum of nine cents for other costs. White coats, laundry — office cleaning —"

They had come to the tall apartment house and were parked. Dick looked up at the higher windows. "I'll finish this quickly," he said, "and we'll go up. I've still the office payroll, which should need no explanation. After deducting all these expenses, I think sixty-three per cent is left for me as pre-tax profit for my work and expertise. A bit short of a hundred thousand."

As he did tonight with Mrs. Baus, he got out of the car, taking a large envelope and his bag with him. Reed had offered to carry them. "Thank you for explaining to me," he had said, his tone uncertain. They went into the building and gave their names and purpose to the security man who sat behind a desk there.

"There are variations," Dick said. "Some doctors are in debt for loans secured during their training. I know of a pediatrician working in an area such as my wife wants me to adopt — he made thirty-five thousand dollars and held two jobs in addition to his practice."

Reed whistled softly. Had Dr. Foster told his wife that? They went into the elevator, and talked no more about a doctor's income.

Tonight Dick and Alice Baus saw their patient, they talked to the family and at the end of an hour they had secured an agreement for the woman to enter Research Hospital and become the patient of a surgeon with whom Dr. Foster worked. Baus. Crans. Dick kept remembering that other evening when Crans had been his companion. Then too the husband had said, "Even if it doesn't help much, we'll know we have done all we could. You'll keep in touch with us, Dr. Foster? My wife trusts you."

As they drove home, Reed Crans had asked if Dick would charge for a house call.

Dick laughed. "I'll get an attending physician's fee," he explained. "The surgery will cost a thousand dollars."

"How long . . . ?"

"At the table? Two hours, three. Preparation, postoperative care — his studies and the learning of expertise. A thousand is not too much."

"If one can afford it."

"We both do charity work," said Dick mildly.

"Another cut of the pie?"

"That comes under the nine-cent 'other costs.' "

Reed offered to put the car away and close up. "I want my father to meet you," he told his docent. "Would you accept an invitation to dinner? With Mrs. Foster, of course. I know my parents . . ."

Dick shook his head. "I want to know them, too. But not when someone might think you were offering an apple to the teacher."

Crans had looked shocked. "Oh, I didn't . . ."

"I know you didn't," Dick said quickly. "But think about the matter before you go to sleep tonight. Of course your parents, any member of your family — if we are at home, they are welcome to drop in."

Reed smiled. "I can go to sleep almost at once," he said. "Do you know? We have a People to People woman living with us this year? She's from Austria, and very interesting. You should have heard my explaining my connection with you."

On Saturday afternoon — it was a beautiful spring day with hundreds of jonquils blooming up on the wooded slope behind their houses — Dick went over to his brother's home, telling Crans he could do as he wished. "Maybe I can scare up a tennis partner for you," he said. "My sister-in-law's family swarms with kids of all ages. Some of them are sure to be there."

"Do you want me to play tennis?"

Dick looked puzzled. "I want you to do anything you like. This for me, as it is for you, is a rest time. Just stay in touch, in case I get called out. Jackson used to sleep. Alice Baus says she washes her hair."

Crans laughed. "I think I'll tag along with you, if the family won't mind."

"Of course they won't mind. My brother — I've explained about his heart and his forced inactivity. He gets bored, and somewhat depressed. Feels unneeded. Which is nonsense, and must be combated. Come along, you'll enjoy the zoo."

Dick enjoyed them, Crans could see. He joked with the children, and put an arm about his brother's shoulder.

"He's taking my pulse," Gene told the young student.

"He's a smart doctor," said Crans.

"That's the way to get along with him," agreed Gene. They walked around the yard, and Gene told how the jonquils had been planted. There was a problem with one row of Dick's roses. Gene had a vegetable garden. "And rabbits," he declared. "They even eat my pansies."

Finally the men settled in chairs on the

flagstone patio behind the houses, and Gene's wife, Marlene, brought out lemonade and ginger cookies. Marlene was a somewhat overweight, tall, motherly woman, about as different from Jan Foster as a woman could be. No, she told Crans, none of the children were hers. "But nieces, nephews — I've lost count." She glanced across to where Dick sat beside his brother. "Gene is the businessman of the family," she told her young visitor. "He takes care of Dick's personal business as well as ours. Now, I'll try to sort out the families. I have six sisters and brothers, you know. And they all breed like rabbits except me. But that was Gene's fault. We didn't settle down and get married until we were both forty."

She chattered along, and brightened perceptibly when still another car drove in. "That's Lindsay," she said. "Lindsay Tabler, a nephew. He's gone into Gene's business and we think he will eventually head it. He had two brothers. One was killed in Viet Nam; he had planned to be a career soldier. The other brother won't even take advice. Lindsay and his wife have two little girls; one has a brain disease. That's sad. And there's a sister, too. Joan. She's more like Lindsay . . . Yes! There she is, the redhead."

"Wow!" said Reed Crans.

Marlene Foster laughed, and pressed his knee. "I'll get more lemonade. Go introduce yourself."

Crans had had a fine afternoon, he told Dick two hours later. "Your brother's wife loves all those kids, good and bad."

"So does Gene. And they want to do for them. He's taken Lindsay into the business. They sell road machinery, and the fella seems to be picking it up very quickly. He's married, has the two children. Gene feels very encouraged that he'll have Lindsay to carry on. It makes for a satisfactory setup, and gives Gene hope that his work and his life will be continued."

"What's his wife like?"

"Lindsay's? Oh, she's the average young woman. She's all right."

"I enjoyed Joan."

"Yep, Joan is another good one. They have a few rotten apples. Lindsay has a brother —"

"What's wrong with *him?*"

"Nothing, maybe. He takes backpack hikes into the mountains, lives all winter in a wood cabin he built up in the Sawtooths. Joan teaches school."

"She's pretty. Do you think they'll be around for my father to meet if he comes to see me at your home?"

"Tomorrow, you think?"

"I told him he could. I think he and your brother will like each other."

"The man hasn't been born who doesn't like Gene. It's a rotten shame his heart played out and he can't —"

As he spoke he had been assuring himself that he would make every effort to have Reed's parents meet Gene's family. If the father was as smart as his son, he'd "read" Jan, and Gene and Marlene, Lindsay and Joan —

He spent that evening thinking about his "family." Gene with an "old" wife who could not have children of their own. Dick, a young man with a young-enough wife who wouldn't have them.

Sometimes he wondered what sort of mother Jan would make. A rigid disciplinarian? A fond and foolish —

Oh, there was no point in speculating. He'd go work on his doll houses.

Chapter 4

On that Sunday evening Dick thought that the weekend had been a good one. On Sunday morning, he and Reed Crans had made hospital rounds. Early in the afternoon, Reed's parents dropped in. Pleasant people, solid citizens. Reed looked like his mother, dark and smiling. Mr. Crans was the typical broker in his dark blue silk suit; he was balding a little and still somewhat confused at the turn his son had taken in his life. Did Dr. Foster think Reed would make a good doctor?

Dick laughed. "For what my opinion is worth, he'll make a fine doctor. He likes people, and cares about what happens to them. That really is what it takes."

Crans had taken them to meet Gene and Marlene, and Mr. Crans was more at home with the manufacturer than he had been with the doctor. But all in all, it was a pleasant interlude. Joan Tabler had stayed all night with the family; Lindsay came in about three. He lifted a knowing eyebrow to see his sister and Reed going up the hill "to look at the jonquils."

"Joan gets them every time," he told Dick. "She's a popular girl."

"Well, young Crans is something special, too."

"Are his parents checking on you?"

"I don't think so. He wanted them to come and meet me, and see where and how he was living."

"Have they met Aunt Jan?"

"Of course. But she didn't want to come outside. I forget the excuse she made."

Lindsay said nothing. They all knew Jan; they felt sorry for Dick, but tactfully the situation was scarcely ever spoken of, and never to Dick. He must know anything that they would say.

Lindsay was a fine young man, smiling and friendly. His thick hair was a darker red than Joan's, but he had her same ease with people, the same ability to make friends. He and Reed Crans had hit if off immediately, Crans commenting on the fact that Lindsay worked as hard as a doctor, no Saturday or Sunday afternoons off.

"It's the only chance I get to come out here and pump Uncle Gene for information. I save up all the problems of the week, bring them here; he tells me what I should do or say, and on Monday I go back to the plant office full of wisdom and good judgment."

There was a deal of comment on this — some argument, some teasing. A great deal of enjoyment. It turned out to be a fine weekend, Dick told himself, getting drowsy. The sunshine, the flowers — a sleepy baby cuddled in her mother's arms, three little girls playing jacks on a flat stone of the patio, a somewhat noisy game of catch out on the sunny lawn.

And when he and Crans showed up at the office on Monday morning, Leslie could see that the weekend had gone well.

"I hope you are ready for a schedule with a capital *S*," she warned them.

"Ready or not, there's always one waiting for me," said Dick. He told about the hip replacement.

Yes, she had a consultation on that for the next day. "How did you manage that?"

"Pure charm," said Dick.

"Mixed with some threats and dire predictions."

"All in the patient's interest."

"Provided she sticks to her post-op therapy," said Leslie, smiling at Reed Crans.

"She will," the student told her. "The doctor cracks a mean whip."

Dick, a bundle of pink slips in his hand,

hurried toward his office, Crans close behind him. The waiting room was full, and a busy morning followed. Dick's "syphilis" patient showed up; Dick handed her record folder to Crans to study. He would need to explain to this student as he had to Jackson and would to Alice Baus, that sometimes a little deception was a good pain killer.

Crans accepted this without argument. Baus would not, and Jackson had wanted it used more often.

That day he and Crans had gone quickly to work. A man with an incipient heart condition had had chest pains but had not wanted to bother the doctor on Sunday.

"Doctors are here to be bothered," said Dick.

"But your lab or office would not have been open."

"There are hospitals. And that is where you are going now. How did you get here? Did someone bring you?"

"My wife dropped me off. She went on to work."

"Well, you shouldn't drive anyway. But I do think you can make it in a cab. I want you to enter General Hospital. I'll call ahead and tell them what I want done, and I'll see you later today."

The man was ready to argue. Crans was

delegated to put him in a wheelchair and take him to the cab when it came. "Emergency Room — they'll be waiting," he said.

"Don't those patients scare you?" the young man asked Dick when he returned.

"Yes, and they make me angry, too. I only hope —" He buzzed for the next patient, even as he made notes on the heart patient's card. The patients went through, and Dick put in a full day. During it, Crans was gone for four hours for class work, then joined Dick at General Hospital at three in the afternoon.

"You can study tonight," Dick told him. "Your house or mine. Truesdell has called a docent meeting."

"And I can't attend?"

Dick smiled at him.

"How many students do you have?"

"I have the original six. There have been three dropouts for the other men. Maybe I don't work you as hard."

"Were we recruited?"

"Were you?"

"We were told of the program. I signed up at once. Maybe some of the others were recruited. Jackson perhaps?"

Dick nodded. "One of our women has a biology degree, and was laid off from her job at a chemical company. She applied at a St.

Louis medical school and was turned down, so she decided to enroll here, hoping her year's record would get her in at St. Louis."

"Will it?"

"It might. She finds weekend commuting three hundred miles a hardship. Her husband works in St. Louis."

"He isn't a husband."

Dick shrugged. "It's hard to tell these days, isn't it? But for Truesdell, it might make a difference."

"I'm glad I drew you."

"I think you should have a month with both Truesdell and Utley."

"Yes, Doctor."

Dick nodded.

He would have hated to miss Crans and his two weeks of "pocket" service. He liked the lad. After Alice Baus, Dick was going to claim a month free before taking on Wellinghof, whom he always thought of as Uriah Heep. The fellow was on a grant, he did well in his scholastic studies. He resented Crans, or any of the students who could afford schooling.

And the first thing he would ask Dr. Foster, the first thing he did ask him, was the earning possibilities of a primary doctor.

Crans had asked, and not been resented. But Wellinghof—

"During medical school you will be sure to find your direction," Dr. Foster assured the fellow now. "You can't start out where I am after ten years."

Jan did not like Leroy Wellinghof. He had long hair which he gathered into a sparse ponytail, and he was a vegetarian.

"Cook what you usually serve," Dick answered Jan's questions. "He can find enough to eat to avoid starvation."

"But —"

"I am definitely not a vegetarian!"

"Don't you have two more of these students?"

"I'm afraid so."

"Are any of them normal?"

"What is normal, Jan? You? Me?"

"You always have to get personal."

Of course he did. That was his job as docent. He met with his six students, singly, and as a group as often as he could arrange such meetings. But he was busy, and so were they, with their college prep work, their wish to find a summer job, their personal interests. Dick wondered if he were handling these problems as well as did Truesdell and Utley. He supposed their groups were not too different. Six young people, their lives intertwined . . .

He pointed this out to his group.

"Our lives are mixed up with yours, too, Big Doc," said one of the men. McDonald.

"Heavens!" said Dick. "I hope not!"

"Why?" asked Jackson. "Do you have secrets?"

"Not really," said Dick. "But I don't want complications because of the work I am doing with you chaps."

"That's fair enough," said Crans.

"We don't want them either," said Jackson in his manner of swaggering when he only spoke and did not move.

Dick worried about Jackson. He could make his M.D. and become what Dick called an opportunist medic. In training, he sent out feelers with which to suck in —

"Oh, stop it!" he told himself aloud. Unless he meant to write such guff into Jackson's final report, he'd better not think about it, either.

But if the program was going to work . . . Was it? Even this far into it, he did not know. Because, to be honest, what "program" did work? One could plan and crosscheck, and plan again, but from simple to complex, what did "work"?

An idea happened. Someone had had the idea for the docent program, then, with each student the program developed quirks. Exceptions had to be made, compensations considered, direction changed.

And perhaps this truth about planned programs was a good thing. A marriage, theoretically, was a planned thing. A man's life was. Dick's had so started.

He had decided, while still in his parents' home, that he would be a doctor and then — He really would be shocked if he thought for one minute that he had *planned* his life as it now stood.

This was not the first nor even the hundredth time he had considered this. And inevitably he ended — when not interrupted — by asking if he should let things go as they were doing? It was not what he wanted, really, but it was easier than the alternatives which presented themselves. He had achieved a quiet acceptance. In his marriage, he had made a mistake, and then lived with it for a dozen years. Not happy, but engrossed in his work, in the people he met and with whom he worked, in Gene's family and his problems.

But anyone looking on at his life must think, and Gene sometimes said, that Dick should fight Jan. Make her do the things Dick wanted — or —

But the very term used shocked him.

He was not essentially a *fighting* man. That Dick Foster did know about himself. A better description was that he conducted a steady march along the way his feet had been set. His work, and his personal life. When he made a mistake, he paid for it, and went on. There was a certain pride in having done this.

But occasionally he would find himself looking at Jan as she busied herself with some sewing or coupon clipping and he told himself that, really, he should consider her side of their relationship.

Perhaps she wanted sex. Perhaps she even wanted children. He had not asked, and she had not said. Perhaps she hated their home on which she had spent so much real effort.

She said she would be happier living in a small town, on a small farm. But would she be? If Dick were really discontented and frustrated, he might not be the calm man he now was, adjusting himself to their way of life.

So, was he to blame? He had given Jan a fine home, and in the suburbs where she could have a garden and simulate small-town living. He had on many occasions tried to share his friends with her. She seldom accompanied him on trips to medical meetings. She would seldom join the family at Gene's and never invited the family to their house. He had tried to share with her the medical successes he had received. Now she said she would not go to any meeting where he would speak or be recognized. Questioned about this position, she came up with the explanation that he was always introduced as Dr. Richard Foster, a successful primary doctor who had done this or that, developed something or other, and then there would be the addition, "and Mrs. Foster, his wife."

This she called being second fiddle, and perhaps Dick would not have liked it either. Though he saw other wives, lovingly proud of their husbands and their achievements.

And "second fiddles" were a necessary part of any orchestra.

He had urged Jan to be "busier." That word had turned her cold. Angry. Didn't he think keeping a large house, tending a garden, kept a woman busy? He said he still thought she could find satisfaction doing volunteer work. In the medical field, or driving for the Red Cross. She did join the Auxiliary, and made trouble which, to say the best of it, occupied her mind. She chose to turn down the Red Cross chauffeur job with the specious argument that there was no need for her to pre-empt anyone's paid job.

Dick had planned to explain to her about

the volunteer service; she would be most welcome if she would enjoy the work.

She thought she would not.

So after some thought — this was before the docent program — he had studied what her interests were. And offered to join the rapid reading class, and after that, the one studying Italian. That had not worked either. He had made friends, Jan had not. Once, at the end of a long day, he had fallen asleep.

She refused to finish that course of classes. His fault, of course. He was sorry, and their classmates laughed and protested their leaving the class.

But Jan would not be persuaded. The doctor was attending, she said, only to make her do things she really did not want to do.

There came a certain warm, rainy evening. Dick had worked down in his — Jan called it his playroom — for an hour or so. Now he came upstairs, got his usual glass of milk, and asked about Wellinghof.

Jan shrugged. "Gone to bed, I imagine. Couldn't you make him cut that hair?"

"No, I couldn't. My authority over him is limited."

"I should think his parents . . ."

"I don't know much about his family."

"Well, everybody has parents."

"And parents have children. Jan —"

He went across the room and stood beside her. "Jan, I want children. You know that I do."

She went on with her reading, turning a page.

"At our age," Dick persisted, "we should be starting a family. If ever we are to have one."

She closed the book on her finger. "Are you saying that you will make me — ?"

He turned away. "No. Of course not."

Jan opened her book again. "I would like to have children, too," she said airily. "But not to raise and send to schools in the city suburbs."

Dick stood for a minute looking at her. So that was it? Blackmail. Gene had said she would use it. Kenny had suggested that she would.

He took his glass to the kitchen, rinsed it and put it into the dishwasher. *As I have been trained,* he told himself.

"Since I do work and live in the suburbs," he said, returning to the living room, "perhaps you and I would be better off divorced, and free . . ."

She rose from her chair. "I do not believe in divorce," she said primly. "But get one if you can."

"I can if you refuse to give me children."

"I have not refused."

He still could get the divorce, he felt sure. After a dirty court fight, maybe. And he would face that if there were someone else. He went outside and walked up and down in the rain. He wished he were Reed Crans's age, or Lindsay's. He wished he had known, at their age, that one could shape his whole life of misery and happiness with one act and word, one error.

He went to the door. "I am going over to Gene's," he said. "I have my key."

"Okay," said Jan, who was reading again, her head bent over the book. He didn't know what book. He didn't know much of anything about Jan. Except that she would use blackmail.

Gene was glad to see him. Marlene had gone to someone's graduation exercise. There always was someone in the family graduating from something. "What's eating you, Richard?"

Not stopping to think whether he should or not, Dick told what was eating him, ending up with the opinion that Jan was ready to blackmail him.

"What does she want?"

"A small-town practice and some farmland."

"She's been on that kick for years."

"I know that," said Dick, "but when I've offered to give her a divorce and the farmland, she refuses."

"She wants you in on the deal. Why? And don't tell me she loves you."

"She never did love me. She has always wanted the strength of marriage to some sucker of a man . . ." That was strong talk from Dick.

"But you think she would fight you in court?"

"I know she would. Dirty-fight, at that." He mentioned Kenny's warning. "Jackson would help her there. And I'd be my own best, or worst, witness on the family deal."

"Yes," Gene agreed. "You would be."

"Maybe I should give in to her. General and Children's both have Emergency Room doctors on weekends who are small-town medics rounding out their incomes."

"Well, I think you should not let Jan tell you what to do. And I can give you a hundred reasons. But say you did, what would you gain, sonny? Blackmail is about the most nonproductive act I can think of. It only results in more blackmail."

"How . . . ?"

"Look! And I am not getting excited. Say you would go into that country practice she wants for you. You'd be a success. Popular. Busy. And Jan would be jealous. So you would have more whining — more demands. And probably no children. Why do you want her kids, anyway?"

Dick laughed. "They'd be half mine."

"And would inherit all the problems you've had with Jan."

"I've had them, and I haven't handled them very well, Gene. I'm not the man you are, brother. You've met with reverses and handled them. You developed a bad heart, and you had to give up the business you enjoyed and which you had built up. But you found a solution."

"I had Lindsay come in, put on my shoes . . ."

"Yes, you did."

"Which was not the same sort of problem you have, Dick. A good thing I could handle them because I am not as smart, as wise, as you are. In fact, I think it shows I was not. I was contented with Lindsay running my business exactly as I had it going. But you are smart. You constantly go into new things in your profession and no one can take over your brain power, your instincts, your rapport with people, your —"

"Oh, shut up!" said Dick, laughing. "Haven't you guessed that all those things came because in a weak moment I proved that I was human, and subject to failure? I didn't have to marry Jan. I hope Lindsay has been smarter in his selection of a wife."

"Leona? Well — She's given him children. The one, poor thing, and the healthy, fat baby. She will help Lindsay in the office if she is needed. That's where he met her, of course."

"And they get along. That's my weakness with Jan. We neither one seem able to make adjustments the way you and Marlene have done."

For a minute, Gene sat silent. "Adjustments," he said thoughtfully. "I guess we have made them. Because we had to. But I can remember —"

"So can I," said Dick. "I can remember when Lindsay first came to work for you. He didn't know a grader from a back hoe. But he was a pleasant fellow —"

"And the first thing he did was to get married," said Gene wryly.

"You went into a real tizzy about that. He didn't make enough money, he was too young — he had nothing in the world except the job you had made for him. And a baby nine months after he married the girl, a baby that had to mean hospital care —"

"I could see nothing except disaster for

them. Marlene thought we would have to help them along."

"And you did," Dick laughed. "You hit the roof when I told you it all meant progress."

"And I asked you what in hell you knew about it."

"Yes, you did. You didn't, then, think that Leona would be a stabilizing force."

"That was Marlene. She didn't like Leona. The business girl rather than a homemaker. And the fact that you kept urging us to give Leona a chance. She thought you were siding against us."

"There were no *sides*, brother dear. But before we got all that ironed out you came down with the worst coronary I've ever known to hit a man and have him survive. And there you were with Lindsay to fall back on. You'd kept him at your side, training him, explaining to him —"

"I couldn't find anything else for him to do. He wasn't ready to sell, or purchase, or be foreman of the men —"

"But he had been in your office for three or four years, he had gone on trips with you, he knew your contacts personally, he had your own personality, he knew how you filed things — and he had married your secretary."

"Leona, yes. And she worked right along

with him. Not after the second baby came, of course. Whatever Marlene thought, Lindsay's worked out fine."

"Marlene knows that. Whatever he did, or did not do, she realized that I was glad to have him there. He saved the business I was sure I'd have to lose. And that fact alone has given me peace of mind. I know I can trust Lindsay."

"Yes, you can."

The two brothers sat silent for a minute or two. Dick liked the living room of Gene's house, the two long couches that faced each other with the fireplace between them at one end, the scattering of bright cushions, the magazines not too neatly stacked on the coffee table. A used cup left on a small table . . .

"This fellow Reed Crans," Gene said unexpectedly. "One of your students . . ."

"Oh, yes," Dick agreed. "I brought him over here one Sunday afternoon."

"He took quite a shine to Joan, and she's brought him back a time or two. Or three."

Dick was surprised. "Why didn't she bring him —"

"You were gone every time. Have you met Heidi Marie?"

"Heidi?" Dick's head tilted questioningly to one side.

"Yes. She came with them one day. Evening, rather. She's an exchange student living with Reed's parents."

Dick nodded. Crans had told him.

"She's Swiss, or Dutch, or something. Anyway, she's a doll."

Dick laughed. "Crane keeps himself busy."

"I think Joan has his fancy."

"She could do worse. He's a solid person."

"But he plans to study medicine."

"He does. His father is backing him, and I believe there is a trust fund."

"Well, that takes care of another young family," said Gene.

"Are you tired? I could help you to bed."

"Marlene will be coming in. We were talking about Lindsay. I wish he lived close. But she won't hear of it. Leona won't."

"That's right," said Dick. "I admire her for taking the stand. Though if Jan has her way and takes me to the boondocks, I'd let her and Lindsay use my house."

"That's not apt to happen."

"No, it isn't. At least for the rest of the year I have the docent program tying me right here."

"You began in the early spring —"

"Yes, and I'll have to make a six months' report in September. That is going to be a session."

Chapter 5

It was a session, and during the summer, the planning of it preoccupied a lot of Dick's thoughts. He talked about it to Kenny, he discussed it with the students. Harold Jackson and one of the others didn't think it would be important.

"It might mean a student's being dropped or continued in the program," Dr. Foster said. "And that result can certainly affect your entry to medical school."

"Then I sure hope Big Doc makes us out pretty good."

"Big Doc" was not sure he would or could. He was not sure that he should make the report at all. Perhaps the students themselves should speak, or one of them selected by the others. There was a lot to think about.

"Can we be there?" asked Crans.

Dr. Foster didn't know. If not, he would give a full report.

"What about Jackson?" Leslie asked him.

"What about any of them? I hope I won't have to be the first on the docket."

"Won't you need a secretary?"

He smiled at her. "I'd like to have a secretary," was the best answer he could make.

He would ask the Director to let the students make their own reports. This was voted down by Truesdell. "They'd be biased," he claimed.

Dick and Dr. Utley thought the reports would be if the docents alone made them. Dick worked himself into a temper worrying about the report. He put off taking a vacation until the thing was over. He made Kenny promise to attend. "You were allowed to share with me."

"What about Sister's claim that Jackson hangs around the hospital?"

"I may bring it up in meeting," said Dick. "If the students are present. She says he presumes on his privileges. I myself have caught him coming down the stairs."

"And you asked . . ."

"He said he used the toilet up there. How can one prove differently?"

Kenny shrugged. "And the strange sounds the nurses hear?"

"Especially during a hard rainstorm," Dick completed. "I consider that a matter for the hospital's security."

"Tell Sister so!"

"I did. And I told Jackson that he must

not go into Research or hang around this office and building unless so assigned by me."

"Did it work?"

"I told him that last week."

"Hmmnnn."

And finally the details of the report meeting were given to the three docents. The date, the first week in October.

"I hope I get a call," said Dick.

"If you do," said Kenny, "I'll take it for you."

"You would, wouldn't you?"

This was to be a dinner meeting, held at General Hospital, and it would last, it was hoped, three hours. The students could attend, but only as listeners.

The doctors would make their reports as general or detailed as they liked. Each would be given an hour, and questions and discussions would be expected. Yes, names could be used but were not required. They would report in an order chosen by lot.

And finally the dreaded evening arrived. Dick discovered that dinner was not planned for the students, and he ordered some served. Whose fool idea was it that . . . ?

"You've found the sour note pretty quick, haven't you?" Kenny told him.

"I didn't have to look far."

The meeting was being held in the staff dining room, and the meal served was "not worth all that fuss." About half the students showed up. Most of Dick's did, Jackson prominent among them. "He won't be a listener," Dick assured Kenny. His fork pushed the meat loaf around on his plate.

Truesdell was the one chosen to speak first. He gave a general report. The program only bothered him in his work, he declared. And he doubted if the students were learning much. He would advise discontinuation of the practice of taking the students into the home. Three of his students had withdrawn. Two from lack of interest in premedicine, and one because he had developed hepatitis and felt that this six weeks of inactivity would be a handicap.

Dick nodded. It would be that. He was studying the students as they ate their meat loaf, scalloped potatoes, green beans, and pineapple salad. "Typical hospital fare" he called it when he got up to speak. Only one of his six had not shown. "I don't know if this meeting was a good idea or a bad one," he said. "I could say the same thing about the docent program. I hope some good comes from the whole idea. It is obvious that the American public needs adequate primary care from the doctors whose referrals are needed and who can learn to know all aspects of their patients. Family practice supplies that kind of care. It is my specialty and what I have accented to my students."

"You can get into some funny arguments on that point," said Utley.

"I can," agreed Dick, "and I do. People say that family practice is shrinking and so it does no good to offer programs geared to it. But the discussion for this hour needs to stay on the point that the public is in dire need of family care.

"Now — I have made, ready to hand to you, detailed reports on each of my students. It includes everything from their attendance records to the state of their health. I shall introduce these students as the reports are passed around. Then I expect to answer questions from my colleagues, or even from some of the students."

His manner and his appearance were pleasant. He had secured the attention of his small audience.

"How has the colored boy been received by the patients in general?" asked Truesdell.

Dick bit his tongue. "Mr. Jackson happens to be black," he said coldly. "He is a bright fellow and can go the course if he wants to. He has some problems, but so do some of the others. Wellinghof's long hair,

Mrs. Baus's obvious femininity. I think a great deal depends on the field Jackson chooses in determining his chances for success. He is alert and curious to learn, especially the strange ways of white *boys*."

There was a murmur of approval. Jackson's teeth flashed.

"You had to throw the egg in the fan, didn't you?" murmured Kenny.

"Tell us about the girl," said Dr. Utley. "Does she have problems?"

"If she doesn't," said Dick, "she is the only one connected with our medical situation."

He turned around in his chair. "Mrs. Baus," he asked, "will you stand for a moment?"

She did stand. A slender young woman, blond; she was wearing a white jacket.

"Have you had problems because you are planning to be a doctor?" Dick asked her.

"None that couldn't be handled," said Alice Baus quietly. "It's usually the women who think other women should not try for a medical degree."

"In the hospitals?"

"Everywhere."

Dick nodded. "Will you tell my colleagues how you happened to decide on medicine? Just what you told me?"

"Yes, sir. I had earned a degree in biology

in one of the state colleges. And I got a job with a chemical company in St. Louis. My husband still works there. The project on which I was working was discontinued. It was one of those Government-order things. On the spur of the moment I applied for admission to one of the medical schools and was turned down with the suggestion that my best hope would be with the new medical school being planned and built here in this city. My record was pretty good, and I was accepted in the school, and for the docent program."

"Thank you, Alice," said Dr. Foster, immediately wishing he had not used her first name.

"You found working with Dr. Foster pleasant?" asked Dr. Truesdell.

Good Lord! The man didn't want blacks or women doctors!

"Of course it was pleasant," Alice Baus was asserting firmly. "He is a pleasant person to work with."

Kenny groaned softly.

"Do you plan to stay in our school?" asked Dr. Utley.

"Well, attending classes eleven months out of the year, and often duty on Saturdays," said Mrs. Baus, "makes commuting difficult."

"Yes, it would. What are your plans?"

"I am not sure, sir. At first I hoped that if I did well here this year, got my pre-med record in good order, I would reapply at the St. Louis school and probably get in."

"But now?"

"I probably won't want to transfer."

"Because of Dr. Foster?"

"Because of the real interest he has shown in what I've done and will do."

Good Lord! thought Dick. She is really setting things up for Truesdell.

Yes, she was. "He has even offered," said Alice Baus, "to take me with him when he goes out of town on consultations."

"Do you go?"

"I did once. He had to go to Topeka for a former patient with celiac disease. You see, as a child, it was thought that I had this problem — it was called nontropical sprue. When this former patient was trying to persuade her doctor that she did not need intestinal surgery, Dr. Foster was ready to produce records and other testimony —"

Her voice thinned. Dr. Truesdell, a tall, thin man, had risen from his chair and was leaning across the table toward her. "Are you telling me that Dr. Foster took you across state lines?" He spoke roughly.

Dick was on his feet, Kenny tugging at his

coat. “See here, Truesdell!” cried Dr. Foster. “I know what you are getting at, and I can tell you —”

“I think the matter should be referred to the authorities,” said Truesdell righteously. The Director was calling for order. The room was pretty well in a turmoil, everyone talking at once. With the state line going through the city, why shouldn’t he have driven Alice Baus across that line?

“Truesdell,” Dick shouted, “you are out of your mind!”

The Director was still asking for quiet. “This seems to have become a serious matter,” he said firmly. “On the face of it, I would say a ridiculous charge has been suggested if not made. Dr. Truesdell, you were not seriously considering . . . ?”

Truesdell was sulking. “I have made no charges. I just think the problem of women medics gets out of hand, and will tend to do so. You might ask Foster how long they were in Topeka, what they did there —”

Smiling a little, the Director turned to Dick. “Doctor, how long were you in Topeka?”

“You know how long it takes to drive there. We attended the consultation and Mrs. Baus answered questions. I bought her food. I think a tuna sandwich. I had my usual club. We drove home. And if anyone thinks we dallied between these activities, he is forgetting what a thoroughly married man I am."

Except for a few of the students, everyone did know Jan. Dr. Utley asked Alice Baus if she had fully recovered from her sprue.

"I can't eat wheat," she said.

"Are you a good student?"

"It's on the record sheet I gave you," Dick answered for her. "I would, at this point, recommend her. Especially for the research area of medicine. But yes, she is a good, average pre-med student."

"Pretty, too," said one of the students.

"Average there as well," Alice reproved him.

Truesdell was asking for the floor. The Director protested in the interest of time.

"This won't take a minute. I simply want to move, suggest, whatever it takes, that Foster's little escapade should not become a matter of practice for the docent doctor. I don't think it should be repeated."

"And I don't agree with you," said Dick. "It was not an escapade. Your order would be ridiculous."

"It is not an order," the Director reminded him. "I think we are now ready for Dr. Utley's report."

"I don't think we are ready," said Dick,

standing. "I want to know if Truesdell is setting himself up to be a watchdog of the docents. If he has been that, I have not been accorded the same privilege. As for this meeting, I thought it was called to evaluate the progress of the program. But I think we can decide right now that it is in trouble. Truesdell doesn't like it, and he seems capable of scuttling it in any way he can."

Heads turned, for one of the students had risen and was coming toward the table where the doctors sat. "I believe it can be proven," said Reed Crans, "that Dr. Foster is right. You could and perhaps should, question Dr. Truesdell's students. Or you could question us, the ones in Dr. Foster's group. We think we are learning, and doing better. We are shown cases, and he discusses them with us. He specifically instructs us on ethical behavior. I understand Dr. Truesdell does little but hold class sessions, so our way is better."

"But there shouldn't *be* any better!" said Kenneth Harrington. "I supposed all three segments —" He broke off because the intercom was sounding. "Attention Code Three. Attention Code Three. Will Dr. Foster contact the office, *stat.* Attention —"

Dick was up and out of the room, leaving the others silenced out of interest, or curiosity, or both. He went no farther than the phone in the hall, and returned almost at once. "Kenny, I'll need you, and I shall not be able to conclude this meeting. A donor has been found for one of my patients on dialysis and —"

The Director and Truesdell looked at Dr. Utley, who shrugged. "I don't get all the urology cases," he reminded them. "Anyway, these things usually come through a good family doctor like Foster." It was his way of saying that he deplored Truesdell's behavior that evening. "Good luck, sir."

Dick was gone, Harrington with him. Crans asked what student . . . ? There was no one assigned for that week. "Then I'm going to follow him," said Crans, running out of the room. He must find out where Dr. Foster had gone, where the surgery would take place —

"He may still be in the house," said the nurse at the desk. "On the phone. He has the family, the patient to notify, the hospital O.R."

"Was there an accident?" asked Crans.

"I imagine so."

"I hope they determine if it was an actual brain death," said Dr. Truesdell, coming out of the meeting room.

"He's a real nasty, isn't he?" asked Crans.

"Yes, he is," she agreed. "You students

can learn a lot from his sort."

"Mr. Crans?" the Director was calling from the meeting room. "Dr. Utley would like all students to return."

"But —"

"You can catch up with Foster later. I think you will find what Dr. Utley has to say interesting and informative."

It was both. The surgeon called it an impromptu lecture to the students about what had happened and probably was happening. "Dr. Foster would do this much better than I can," he warned the group of students. "But this does come into my field. You see, evidently Dr. Foster has a patient with failed, or seriously failing, kidneys. That patient is on the dialysis machine waiting for a suitable transplant. I would guess that there has been a serious accident in this area, and Dr. Foster's need being on file, if the victim has died, or is about to die, and has the proper qualification of health, blood type, all the necessary things, the operation can be done as quickly as all the participants can be gathered together. Patient, donor, donor's family — surgical team. Speed is needed, and an efficient meshing of services."

"Will they do it here?" asked someone.

"I don't know. We'll be able to find that out at the desk."

"It's exciting," said one of the men.

"Medicine can be very exciting," agreed Dr. Utley.

"Will Dr. Foster do the transplant?"

"Oh, no. He's not a surgeon. His service has been in meeting the patient, diagnosing his need, setting lines out by which a transplant team will serve this person. Evidently a donor has shown up. This donor's family must be reached, and quickly, then the urologist and his team will take over."

"You're a urologist, sir."

"I am, and I do transplants. But I am not in on this one. However, I do want to emphasize the importance of doctors like Foster and Harrington, who see these patients and their needs, and set up help and very likely cures for them. Now, we'll adjourn. The Director has departed and I assume the meeting is over."

"And you've done a lot to counteract what Dr. Truesdell tried to do to Dr. Foster," said Alice Baus.

Dr. Utley flushed. "We have to learn to handle such things," he said quietly. "Good night, gentlemen. And that includes you, Mrs. Baus."

After that meeting Dr. Truesdell withdrew from the docent program, and Kenny

Harrington took over his three remaining students. Dick agreed that he should, but it made things rather too busy in his own practice. It was agreed that the students could make the long Christmas break without needing to report to their docents. "I can now break my neck catching up on my own work," Dick told Leslie.

"Why don't you go to Florida or Bermuda?"

"Jan —"

She smiled at him, and he shook his head at her. "Marlene and Gene want the whole family at their house for Christmas Day," he said. "And I understand that Jan has agreed to bake and decorate old-fashioned cut-out cookies with which to trim the tree."

"She has?"

"She is a very good cook and often makes those rabbits and gingerbread men for Christmas. Of course the tree project would take a lot of cookies."

"Is Gene able . . . ?"

"I brought that up and he informed me he wanted to do what he enjoyed doing as long as the Lord would permit. He says he won't get overtired, and I can understand his wanting the family all together."

"So can I. And I would like to see the cookie-trimmed tree."

So would the family. Marlene got the tree set into place; she asked Jan how the cookies were coming along. "They don't have to be day-old fresh. Can't some of us help ice them?"

Jan said only that she would manage. And manage she did. On the morning of Christmas Day, with the tinsel-garlanded tree awaiting the gay little sugared Santas and wreaths and horses, Jan called Marlene.

"The cookies aren't working out," she said airily. "I'm sure you'll think of a substitute." And she hung up the phone.

"Well, at least she didn't wish me a Merry Christmas," said Marlene, sitting stunned at the breakfast bar. Slowly she put the phone back on its rest.

"What's happened?" asked Gene. "You look — funny."

Marlene sprang to life. "Well, I'm damned if I feel funny!" she cried.

"Hey, *hey!*" Gene protested.

Marlene began to cry. She went swiftly to Gene's side. "You are not —" she began. "You're to let me get mad, and go around in circles. You go in and watch Captain Kangaroo and I'll figure out the best way to kill Jan Foster."

"Now, now," said Gene. "That really would excite me. A murder trial. Come on, sweetie, tell me what it's all about."

Weeping, breaking off to say what she thought of Jan, Marlene finally told him. Marlene was a somewhat plump woman, tall. She had silvery white hair which she wore drawn into a knot on top of her head. Dignity and poise were her best qualities. Then she could be handsome. But a tear-swollen face, and her neat housedress twisted out of shape by her agitated hands no, she was not very attractive, and she knew it. She had done her share for Christmas, she told herself. Turkey, mince pies, the house — Leona was doing the salad and cranberry relish. The least Jan could have done was to tell her a week ago —

"I can't get all those ornaments down from the attic today!" she cried. "I've promised to do some work at the church. Oh, Gene, let's just leave town."

He sat turning a bolt of red ribbon in his hands. "No tickets," he reminded her. "And it's the Today show I watch in the morning. It's educational and I need that." He came to her and kissed her. "But I might try Captain Kangaroo." He looked down at the ribbon in his hands.

"Hey!" he said. "Look. I've made a bow. It's right pretty, isn't it?"

Marlene washed her face with cold water.

"Blubbering like a baby," she scolded herself. She reached for the bow. "Yes, it is pretty," she said."Let's put it on the tree."

They went into the family room where the tree stood. The bright red bow bobbed up and down perkily. "Why can't we . . ." said Gene. "If I can tie a bow, the kids can. There should be a lot of ribbon about."

"Don't call anybody," said Marlene. "They'll be dropping by. Could we use gold ribbon?"

"Sure. Any color. And you put the stuff on the table. I'll tie up a stack of bows while you do your church work — and don't stop and tell Jan what we think of her. There isn't time."

"No, and don't tell Dick what has happened either," said Marlene, going to fetch her coat and her car keys, as well as to snatch a quick glance at her hair.

Gene worked contentedly; some of the children did come by, and eventually Lindsay, who could be told what "that Jan had done to Marlene."

"So we're tying ribbon bows."

Lindsay laughed. "I'm glad to know you hadn't all gone bonkers," he said. "Where is Marlene?"

"At the church. They have all sorts of jobs there, and she thought she had this morning free. Get yourself a beer and I'll make you the target of all I think and have been holding in about Jan."

Lindsay laughed and did as Gene said. No, he hadn't brought any problems from the office. He just thought Marlene might need some help. "She's taken on a big job for today."

Gene pounded his fist on the arm of the chair.

"Hey!" cried Lindsay. "Take it easy. Have you told Uncle Dick?"

"He won't be one bit surprised." He leaned toward Lindsay. "Why doesn't he kill that woman?" he asked angrily.

Lindsay glanced down the room to where three girls were busy with the bow tying. "I'll put the high ones on," he called. Then he turned back to Gene. "Why doesn't he divorce her?" he asked, keeping his voice low. "He has grounds."

"And she would make it the dirtiest divorce case that ever struck this town."

"I wish there were another woman."

"There's Leslie, but they wouldn't ever marry. And the whole medical population knows what Jan is, the way she dresses and looks. She won't go to any sort of dinner party with Dick."

"Does he go alone?"

"Sometimes. And he tries to persuade her; she says she can't talk to strangers, and he knows it. She won't go to a cocktail party. I undertook to ask her why, and she says she is either ignored, or some drunk wants to sit on the couch with her and paw at her."

"Do you believe that?"

"No, and Dick doesn't either. We've talked about it. He is popular, and some of this socializing is a part of his profession. He says if Jan gets that sort of treatment, it is her own fault. She goes into a place dead-eyed.

"She keeps a beautiful home but she won't let Dick entertain there. She won't go on trips with him to medical meetings."

"And she wouldn't make the cookies for the Christmas tree. Does Dick know that?"

"Yes. I think she must have called him. Anyway, he called here and said he was sorry, that he would have some gift shop come out and decorate the tree. I reminded him that it was Christmas morning, and he said he was sorry. He sounded that way too. He was making hospital rounds, he said. I told him that we were managing."

"I think the woman's sick."

"I do, too, and I really think that is why Dick does nothing about a divorce."

Lindsay considered that. "It would make

things very sticky," he agreed. "Have you talked this way to Dick? Uncle Dick?"

Gene smiled. "*Dick* does fine. I've told him that I thought Jan could use a psychiatrist. He said that might be, but if she seemed ready to do it, he would know that his marriage was in trouble."

"Why? Because she would lie?"

"Oh, the shrinks expect that. But Dick remembers that his marriage was in trouble from the first. Our mother told him it was, and that he should not go through with it. I recall she was a real lady, Lindsay, our mother, but she knew what went on in the world. She told him that if every man married the first girl he slept with, the whole world would be in the mess he was cooking up for himself. Dick remembers that."

"Yes," said Lindsay thoughtfully. "And evidently Jan does too."

Christmas developed into a noisy, happy day at Gene's house. The twins loved their doll houses. Leona said, and Dick overheard her, that he — Dick — was creating a fantasy world or home such as he did not have.

Was that true? Probably. Though he did enjoy his miniaturizing. He went home with a bright green bow in his hair, and the wrapped gifts for Jan stacked in his arms. He put them on the kitchen counter, and they were still there, unopened, when he departed for Baltimore and the seminar that he was to attend, and where he would speak on the molested child. He had in the past couple of years gained a good deal of renown because of testimony he had given in court, articles which he had published in medical and lay magazines.

When he mentioned the trip to Jan, she said that he should send Kenneth.

He turned with a small stack of underwear in his hands. "Why?"

"Because I don't like to be left alone."

That was nonsense. Dick suspected that she enjoyed having the house to herself.

"If you're afraid," he said quietly, "you can go over and sleep at Gene's."

She went on down the hall without commenting on his suggestion.

At the office, lining things up with Kenny, he said casually that he was taking Leslie with him. There would be a Kelly girl to fill in.

"I'm glad you'll have company. Tell Leslie to leave her shorthand book at home."

"She will."

"Did you ask Janice to go?"

Dick shook his head. "This time, no," he said, stacking files.

"This time," said Kenny speculatively, "there might be some hope for Dr. Foster."

Dick did not flick an eyelash. "We'll see what sort of presentation I'll make."

"To whom?"

Dick went out and shut the door behind him.

The seminar went well, and Dick's share in it was open to the press. As he always did, he began by pointing out that he was a general practitioner, not in any way a psychiatrist or a psychologist. "But I do specialize in people with problems, and where there has been molestation there are almost certainly problems.

"You have already been told and understand the psychological effect of rape upon little girls. They hate and fear men, they become promiscuous — all that.

"I see those results, too, but there are others. There is disillusionment. A child has trusted an adult, never guessing that harm could come of her trust, which has been betrayed. There is another result I meet and try to handle. The sense of guilt when and because the little girl realizes that she found the molestation an enjoyable experience. This often happens.

"I deal with the child, the growing adolescent, and I have come to my office the parent who has suffered the very real trauma of knowing that her child has been molested. These parents often fantasize about the experience; they think of the experience as worse than it actually was. And they transmit their shock and concern to the youngster.

"The child realizes from the parents' reaction that being touched by an adult — they use that expression — is something terrible. And the next step is to decide that he — the child — must be terrible, and he — or she — begins to feel guilty, shamed and degraded.

"Treatment? Well, there must be treatment for all sorts of things. The parents' excitement, repeated questioning, physical examination — experiences that vary from visits to a psychiatrist and the court to the physician.

"The result: bad dreams, restlessness, the tendency to withdraw, hostility, especially to adults.

"Sometimes older children lie and say there has been molestation where there was none. This indicates that that young person was mentally disturbed prior to the particular incident which is causing all the excitement. Sometimes we find that the child who has been molested has known the offender for a long time, and assault has been frequent.

"What can now be done? One thing: have the adult recognize that it is his responsibility to see that affection-seeking behavior does not result in sexual behavior that is erotic and adult.

"And in all cases, be calm, be patient, be understanding."

He answered questions, he discussed cases. And one psychologist asked him why he stayed in general practice. "You seem to get more of my work than I do."

It was a good trip and the three days of rewarding work and Leslie's pleasant company were good for him. He came home ready to take up the reins again and get on with life. A good night's sleep, and — reaching to take his bag from the car, he stopped short. There was someone leaving the house, coming out of the front door, down the walk . . . The door light went out.

Frowning, Dick secured his bag, got his briefcase, his raincoat, and went on to the house through the side door, as he always did. Jan was going up the stairs, to bed probably. "I didn't hear you drive in," she said over her shoulder.

"Your visitor did." Dick realized that he was very angry. The man leaving his house had been Harold Jackson. And he had seen Jan long enough — He glanced up at her. "What did the fellow want?" he asked.

"His comb. He said he had lost his comb, and thought maybe —"

"He never loses his comb. He keeps it tucked into the back of his Afro, like the lowered mast of a ship. I've told him a dozen times to put it into his pocket."

He passed her on the stairs. "Is the house locked?" he asked.

"If you locked the side door."

"It locks itself." He took his bag into his room, then came again to the hall door. "What did Jackson really want?" he asked.

"The comb. And he said he wanted to see you."

"He knew that I was going to be away. Did he tell you what he wanted to see me about?"

"If you're interested —"

"I am interested. I'd like to decide how important his problem was. He has a way —"

Jan leaned against the wall. "Yes, he does have a way. He's a troubled young man. I talked to him, or rather, let him talk to me."

"Yes? Did he want to leave the program?"

Her eyes flared. "No-o," she said. "I thought he might. But he talked mostly about his home and his family. He doesn't have much to build on, Dick."

"I know his circumstances. I would say he has done very well, considering his background."

"He thinks he is in the program only because he is black."

"That's not true. He gets more assistance than some of the other students, and he takes it as his right."

"Isn't it his right?"

"I am neither a sociologist nor a politician, Jan. I take these students that come to me, and do what I can for them. We have some who resent their grants — Oh, *resent* isn't the word."

"They think that all should be on the same basis."

"Which is patently impossible and would be unjust. Crans doesn't need help. Baus doesn't need as much as Wellinghof, who resents the fact that he has to have any."

"In order to study medicine."

"That's it. Though I would not claim medicine as a burning motivation with him. It is a way for him to earn a good living even when he is still in training — if he makes it to internships and residencies."

"Will he?"

Dick shrugged. "I have no way of knowing."

"Is Jackson dedicated . . . ?"

"I shouldn't talk about his motives. He's smart enough, if he would bend his cleverness to the right things."

"Doesn't he?"

"To make people like him and grant him privileges. Not really to learn medicine if you except the matter of abortions. He really digs into that subject. Methods, results, causes —"

"Then he isn't right for your office."

"No, he is not. But it is an obsession with him. He can tell you exactly which of his mother's eleven children should have been aborted."

"Now he knows."

"Yes."

"He felt very strongly about that little idiot girl you wouldn't help."

"I did help her. And she was brain-damaged, not an idiot."

"There's a difference?"

"There is a difference. As for Jackson — I've tried to have him transferred, but with Truesdell stepping out —"

"Can't another staff doctor take his place?"

"We hope so. But the time is half gone. For now we are redistributing Truesdell's students. There has been a big block in the program itself, with a few exceptions I am not being enthused."

The next day he decided to let Jackson bring up the matter of the comb and his visit with Jan. Or even the matter of abortion. Though he was busy enough. "Be away two days, and four days' work piles up," he grumbled to Kenny.

"There are patients who want only you. Though they know, as you must, that you have to have a break now and then."

Dick did know that, and he really did not mind getting back into harness. He cared for all the messages on his desk; he made rounds at the hospitals. Leslie set up an office schedule for him, and he went to work. The woman who had ignored her allergies and had developed diarrhea, the man who had decided to take off weight by the liquid protein diet —

This always raised Dick's blood pressure. He sent both patients across to Research, one to have fluids restored, the other for tests, feeding, and a diet regime. The man raised a row.

At noon, Dick himself went across the street to see how things were progressing. Sister was glad to see him. "I wish some of your patients would learn to read," she said ironically. "We put articles in the papers; other articles show up in every magazine about the dangers of protein diets."

She reached down to a lower drawer in the desk and brought up an envelope from which she shook a bright red comb. Her glance questioned Dick.

"Jackson?" he asked.

"I have no proof. He always has one tucked into his hair."

"Yes. And he thought he had lost it. Last night —"

"He did lose it. I don't know when. But this morning, the cleaning woman found it up on the top floor and brought it to me."

Dick's face went white.

"Go on and swear," said Sister Alphonsus. "Get it out."

Dick laughed, and told of Jackson's coming to his house, and of the conversation the returning husband had had with Jan. "Half of her arguments," he said in a moment of dropping his guard, "are to irritate me. Maybe not to *irritate,* but she does keep up a running argument —"

"That you should move to the country and do family practice."

"I do family practice here. These people seem to need me."

Dick laid the comb straight on the edge of

the Administrator's desk. "I'll speak to Jackson," he promised, "and let him pick up his own comb. He has no business coming here to the hospital —"

"Or to your home, knowing that you are away."

That was true. "You can at least reinforce my order to stay away from the hospital."

"What does he want, Doctor?"

"I don't know. Those two empty floors fascinated him when he was spending the two weeks with me."

"I wish we had never built them. But the Government —"

He waved a hand at her, and departed. They could discuss that for a whole afternoon.

In February, after two weeks of discussion and persuasion, Gene and Marlene Foster drove to Florida. The weather had turned bitter cold in the midwest; there was a lot of snow which Gene kept wanting to push "just from the front walk to the postbox."

"Get him out of here!" Dick urged his sister-in-law.

"He won't stay long."

"Drive in short spells, that should use up nearly a week. Let him dabble his toes in the water —"

"Now, Dick, really!"

"He could. Of course he'll keep his hat on."

But the next day she got Gene's consent, and she packed a bag for each of them. Gene gave Dick and Lindsay and a couple of other close associates minute directions for the care of their property.

"We could go off and leave the doors unlocked and the windows open, and Lindsay or Dick, or both, would look out for things," Marlene reminded him.

"Oh, sure. With Dick fascinated with those new veneers he got in this past week."

"He never neglects you or any other patient."

Gene settled down into the car seat. "I suppose that's true," he conceded.

"I worry about Dick," he told his wife.

She looked at him in surprise.

"Watch the road. Or I'll drive."

That would be the day! He could drive, but since he had had the heart attack he had always found a way of evading the exercise.

"Why do you worry about Dick?" she asked when they had reached their first motel.

"I don't worry about him."

"You said you did. Back there before we crossed the river."

"Oh? Oh, yes, I did. Well, there are all

sorts of reasons to worry. Are you calling back . . . ?"

"This evening. You told him we would."

Gene nodded. "I'm an old fussbudget and you must get sick and tired of listening to me. Let's go get some lunch. Then a nap and a walk. I know the rules, and I don't plan to spoil this trip. I wish one could get a real ham sandwich, not that chopped-up, squeezed-together stuff."

She laughed. "You are a fussbudget. We'll find something."

"I worry about Dick," Dick's older brother said then, "because of the company he keeps. That Jackson fellow coming there to the house when Dick's gone."

Marlene didn't like that either. "And Dick's gone so much."

"He's a busy doctor. And the trips he takes aren't long or frequent. But I wish that fellow would keep away. I've been tempted to tell him so."

"I'll do it."

"That's not woman's work, Marlene."

"No, I suppose it isn't in this situation. And you —"

He held up his hand. "I'm just hoping," he said, "that if I see any smoke puffs coming from next door, I'll keep my cool."

"You wouldn't."

"Dick would. And he does. Over and over again, I am sure."

"Yes, but you are so different."

"You're dead right," said Gene cheerfully. "I didn't remember to do that, did I, when Lindsay up and married?"

"You certainly did not," said Marlene vigorously.

"I know. I made a complete idiot of myself."

"Yes, and worked yourself into a heart attack."

"I'm sorry about that."

"About the attack, we're all sorry. But you've never regretted what you said to Lindsay."

By the next day they had run out of snow, even remnants of it in the valleys. And Gene seemed to be enjoying himself. Marlene thought perhaps he had left the problems of home behind. But around eleven o'clock that morning it was she who spoke unexpectedly, surprising even herself. "Should we try to save Dick?" she asked.

"From what? Jackson?"

"No, I was thinking of Jan, and the way she does. Poor guy. And he's such a dear man."

Gene grunted. "What do you suggest,

dear Abby?" he asked.

"Well, we could tell Janice about Dick and his secretary."

"Ah, no!" said Gene firmly. "Little Janice, as you call her, is capable of anything, including violence. Besides, if the woman has a lick of sense, she knows about Leslie."

Nodding slowly, Marlene drove along the highway. "You're right," she agreed.

"And there's another thing," said Gene, speaking strongly. "I believe firmly that in these situations, a man has to help himself."

For two or three miles, Marlene thought about that. "Do you think he will?" she asked then.

Gene remembered what they had been talking about. "Oh, sure," he said firmly. "Trust Dick."

Chapter 6

It would have both pleased and disturbed Gene and Marlene to know that Dick was beginning to think somewhat seriously along these lines himself. He had often considered the matter of a divorce from Jan. Relaxed laws would make that more easily accomplished, though he would bet that Jan would find ways to make an ugly case of his effort. She would — well, whatever she did, these scandals never helped a doctor's relationship with his patients.

But he knew that there must be some change.

And that change came.

Gene and Marlene stayed in Florida for two weeks, which everyone concerned considered to be a miracle. Gene came back looking well, but complaining of fleas and the high cost of everything. Marlene laughed about this. "He called Lindsay every night," she told. "Then fussed about the phone charges."

"His activities are so limited, Marlene," Dick reminded her.

"I know. I don't let his fussing bother me. But I don't think he should go to this sales meeting."

Dick's attention alerted. "What sales meeting?"

"Oh, it's the usual thing. Big, noisy, and dull. Business is done, of course."

"Can Lindsay do the business part?"

"Of course. Maybe better than he could with Gene to worry about."

"Gene must know that he should not go on such a trip this soon —"

"Yes, and he knows that Lindsay will go and work hard. He does work hard, you know. We are very lucky to have him. He's smart, and he already has learned the business. He does Gene's work, from opening heavy doors for Gene to go through to attending these sales meetings. Sometimes he goes with Gene and helps him. Sometimes, like this one, he goes on alone, and manages very well. You and I have the hard part, holding Gene down here at home."

"It's hard on Gene, too, remember, though I am sure he's a little tired from the Florida trip, and those smoky meeting rooms, the talking and walking he would have to do —"

"Oh, you're right, Dick. You're right."

"When is this trip?"

"We're driving Lindsay to the airport this evening. We'll leave here about five."

"Won't Leona . . . ?"

"Yes, she would rather take him. You can't blame her. But Gene doesn't think of that. Lindsay is his boy. His mouthpiece."

Dick stood thoughtful. Marlene had followed him to the door after he had given Gene a brief checkup, and had told his brother to watch the ball game.

"Does Gene trust Lindsay?" he asked now.

Marlene was startled. *"Trust?"*

"Mhmmmn. Does he entirely trust Lindsay? You see, it would be very bad for Gene to send Lindsay off on these trips if he didn't."

"Oh, but he does. He does, Dick. He's laid out the whole thing with Lindsay, and he knows that Lindsay will do exactly as they have agreed."

"He's lucky. And the best of all, Lindsay is always smiling and pleasant to be around."

"Yes, he is. Of course the day is coming—"

"But meanwhile Gene is the lucky man."

"And for all his stewing, Gene knows that he is lucky. He feels that you are lucky, too, to have Kenneth."

"I am lucky." He bent to kiss Marlene's cheek. "Good girl," he said. "And, having you, Gene is luckier than I am."

She stood at the door, watching Dick go down the walk and across the lawn to his own house. Poor fellow.

She heard, and felt, Gene coming down the hall behind her. "Pennies still buy thoughts?" he asked.

Marlene laughed. "They would if you'd ever pay me."

"You're still blushing because my brother kissed you."

"I know it, and it feels good."

"What were you thinking about?"

"Oh, I was wondering if Dick ever considered burying Jan in the cellar."

Gene nodded. "I'll bet he does. And then he could start over. When do we leave for the airport?"

Of course Lindsay made a successful trip to Chicago. All Gene could find to complain about was that his return plane was an hour late.

"But that wasn't Lindsay's fault," Marlene protested.

"I know it," snapped Gene. "But the boss can't have his employees getting swell-headed."

The tall, bronze-haired young man laughed. "Will you let me go home and see the family?" he asked. "Or do I have to —"

"Marlene's doing the driving," Gene pointed out. "Just leave your sales book with me."

Summer came on them swiftly, with heat, thunderstorms, beautiful starry nights and lovely dawns. Leslie told Dick that he should be planning a vacation, but he shook his head. "Not with the docent problems . . ."

"Don't these students graduate in June?"

"Yes, and most of them will enter medical school in the fall. I have three who are asking to work with me during the summer, but you know that."

"I think they need a vacation, too."

"Once they make medical school, my duties are over."

"You hope. Jackson, too?"

"Oh, I never doubted his making it. Crans, Baus — but Wellinghof did surprise me."

"I wouldn't have him for a doctor."

"I have been steering him toward research because of his personality. The one I would not have —"

"I know. Jackson. I wish we had different names."

"The name doesn't matter. I trust you —

but that fella — he keeps turning into various things that are shady if not criminal."

"The comb."

"Yes. And do you know? He reclaimed the thing without any explanation. Of course he picked it up when Sister was not at the desk. That's what I mean. He's shifty, but smart, too. He never gives me the material for a genuine beef about him. He just does these shady things; perhaps others are implicated. I have told him flatly to stay away from Research Hospital. So what happens? His mother becomes ill. General transfers her to Research for pneumotherapy."

"And her son Harold must go to see her."

"Yes, and looks at me in a way — like a snake. I think he has extra eyelids."

"Doctor, if he could ever be a menace —"

"If he could ever be that, I'd have him out and away from any involvement in medical affairs. But he is clever, and he says I lean on him because of his color."

"You don't."

"I did over that comb affair. And it is his color that makes him wear the damn thing in his — his —"

Leslie laughed merrily. Then she sobered down. "He used to do some shady things here. That month —"

"I know what month you mean. You

should have told me."

"I could never put anything on him. As you say, he has extra eyelids. When I asked Wellinghof if he was raiding the refrigerator, he blushed all over the place and said he was hungry, that he would replace the can of Sego or whatever it was I had missed. But Jackson — I have to carry my purse with me if I leave my desk."

"Lock it in a drawer. Oh, I know. We never had to take precautions, and maybe we don't now. I suspect he has a way of getting in here when we are gone."

"How?"

"Well, the janitor might let him in. He knows he has been connected with us."

"Yes. And when others are implicated, Jackson is twice as hard to detect."

"He thinks he is smarter than any security guard," said Dick. "I told you about the hospital stairs. When his mother was there, I suspected him of smuggling whiskey or wine — maybe *and* wine — to other patients. But his mother was not my patient, and, at that time, I had none on that floor. I did work up a lecture for all prospective medical students on the ethics required of anyone, from aid to chief of staff, not only in their hospital but in one they might happen to visit."

"What did our boy have to say?"

"Nothing. He pretended to sleep through it. But I am going to see if I can develop some first-class detective work on the matter. I'll use you, and Sister Alphonsus — there are others. I do know I am not going to appear to sponsor, or to have trained, a crooked medic."

He gave the matter a lot of thought. Working in his rose beds, bringing bouquets of flowers to his friends — Kenny's wife and a bouquet for Crans to take to his mother. Crans — Reed — still came to the Gene Foster home with Marlene's niece. He asked Dick about marrying. Would he work hard enough if he were preoccupied with a bride?

"With the right bride you would. She'd see to it. And money would not be your problem."

"Joan thinks she should get a job so that we would have our own apartment and not be too dependent on our parents."

"She's a nice girl. You're lucky. I think she would help push you through medical school."

"I am sure she would. I understand Alice Baus is going back to St. Louis."

"She is. But you'll have Wellinghof and Jackson —" Dick was grinning. Then he sobered. “I shouldn’t talk to you about the other students.”

“But Jackson bugs you.”

“He does. And I can’t put my finger on what it is he does or says. Nothing that would warrant an adverse report on him. Crans, will you forget what I am saying?”

“No. I shan’t repeat it, but I do have one suggestion.”

“Good! What is that?”

“Just to remind you that your wife sees Jackson more than you or anyone else does. I — and your brother — don’t like his hanging around here so much.”

“I know he comes, and Jan makes him feel free to come. Well —”

It was an idea. He would not urge Crans to help him or talk to him again about his problems, but he would try to talk to Jan.

He sighed at the thought of doing it, but that evening turned out rainy and he did not work in his basement shop. Instead he gathered some magazines and a book.

He read some, and thought some more, and waited while Jan cleared the dinner dishes and straightened the kitchen to its usual precise order.

But finally she came into the family room and sat on the far end of the couch with some sewing in her hands. She wore a red skirt, a figured blouse, and her dark hair straggled across her forehead.

Dick closed his book on his finger. "Jan," he said, "you've talked quite a lot, haven't you, about Harold Jackson's interests and his wish to be a doctor? I find him hard to understand, and since the time has come for me to make my report on him, I am trying to *know* the fellow better than I do."

"He comes around," she agreed.

"What do you talk about?"

"Oh, we both like baseball —"

"I mean about his medical work, what he's been doing, what he perhaps expects to do."

"Haven't his grades been all right?"

"At school, yes. My report deals with things other than grades. His interest, his learning ability, his probable success as a doctor. In talking to him, would you say he has a genuine drive for medicine? Is there a need for money?"

"I thought he had some sort of scholarship."

"He does. I was thinking of the future. Would he practice with an eye to a big income? Many young doctors do."

"They certainly do," she said, turning the sewing in her hands, "and old ones, too!"

Dick ignored her imputation. "What

about Jackson? Could that be his first objective?"

She did not answer, and he turned to look at her. Her face had become the impervious blank he so often met with Jan. This time he persisted.

"I don't remember," she said finally, "except for the scholarship, that Jackson has talked about money."

But Dick would bet that they had talked about it, and that Jan had slipped him money on occasion. He was not going to help her to "remember." It was at such times that she could be the most irritating. He picked up his book.

"I'm sure he'll work things out," said Jan at last. "He's resourceful. What has he been doing? Filching drugs? Or doing illegal abortions?"

Dick made a sound of disgust, and threw his book toward the table. He went out of the room and down to his basement workshop. If Jan could only realize how much she told him when she thought she was being sarcastic . . .

The next day, during a brief conference with his partner, he mentioned his concern about Jackson. "If he would just do something definite . . ." he growled.

"We know he should not be in medicine,

but he gives us little choice in what we say. I will tell you that once I found him here in the office after hours."

"Much later?"

"Six-thirty or seven."

"What was he doing?" Dick looked angry.

"He had a waiting-room magazine in his hand. When I asked how he got in, he said that he had been waiting for Wellinghof."

"Here?"

"That was his story."

"Story," Dick repeated dryly. "Did you ask Wellinghof?"

"The next day, yes, I did. He said he knew nothing about any arrangement to meet Jackson, that he wouldn't anyway; he didn't like the guy."

"Hmmn," said Dick. "I get the same answers from Jan. I get them."

He did not try to talk to her again, but still she was the one to whom Jackson talked, and if Dick were to get a true line on the fellow . . .

But he was a busy man, and so was really shocked when things began actually to happen. He spoke of the evening to Kenneth, who thought steps should be taken. Dick gave only a vague agreement to that. What would the "steps" be? Anyway, there might be no connection at all with Jackson when the flower beds at the neighboring motel were dug up. They were pretty flower beds, with all sorts of plants — heliotrope, small blooming clove pinks, with the delightful round green things called "hens and chickens" used for a border. The guests, generally, delighted in them and were careful not to walk on the corners and circles they made about the place.

But then there came a morning when the beds were a shambles, dirt scattered, plants gone. Vandalism, said the motel people sadly.

"What goes on here?" yelled Dick Foster when someone showed him the flowers planted, inexpertly, along the walk of the office building, and a large bed of them directly under his windows.

He worked along with the gardener hired by the motel to restore the plants to their own beds. No one thought he had moved them. But among the plants he found a slender, shining trowel similar to the ones he used about his own garden at home. Of course such trowels could be bought anywhere, but when he finished office hours and the work he did, he would see —

At home, the trowel was gone.

"You've misplaced it," said Jan indifferently.

She knew better, Dick knew better. He was as fussy as an old maid about his tools and garden aids.

But he could not prove a thing, and he was called out before eight o'clock to attend a patient who was dying.

The second day he came to the office, preoccupied, to find Leslie preventing the building maintenance man from washing the big window of Dick's ground-floor office. "He's already done your inside door," said Leslie indignantly.

"I don't think Doc did it," said the man unhappily. "But them crazy pictures! They're blue, Mrs. Jackson! We can't have such porno stuff on our building!"

"I only wanted Dr. Foster to see them," said Leslie.

"He ain't that kinda man!"

"I don't think he did them, I don't think he enjoys them," said Leslie firmly. "But now that he's seen them, you can go ahead and wash, but I'm afraid that chalk is going to stain."

"Yes, ma'am," said the janitor unhappily.

"You've got him in no position to talk to the police," Dick assured Leslie.

"Are you going to call them?"

"I'm not but the building supe will." He was angry about the whole episode, which indeed could be the work of irresponsible vandals, and he did not speak of the window painting to Jan. She read of the matter in the newspaper. "They cleaned it up," was all he said.

All this came at a time when he was very busy. On the staffs of three hospitals, intern and resident changes were part of his responsibilities. He had his docents to give some thought to. And he was not only frightened, but annoyed, when still another mishap occurred.

For one thing, he could have broken his neck, or at least fallen on his face — or, yes, watched what his headlights must have shown him when he drove into the garage.

But he did none of those things. He just got fighting mad as he stepped out of his car and turned to start along the short walk to the house, when he stumbled over a large box directly in his path.

His medical bag, a handful of mail, and his keys, went flying. He caught himself against the garage wall, and managed to turn on the lights. "What in the devil?" He must have said that a half-dozen times. But — *what in the devil?* For "what" was a large box — a pretty big one which had contained some things from a pharmaceutical company. Why did that box stand directly in his way? And the damned thing was half filled with medical samples, phials and bottles, small packages of bandaging materials, syringes —

He retrieved his bag, his mail, and gathered up a sampling handful of stuff from the box, then strode off for the house.

"Jan!" he shouted as he came into the short hall. And *"Jan!"* again.

She came down to the landing at the turn of the stairs. Clutching a robe about her, she must have been starting for bed. "What on earth?" she asked. "What are you shouting about?"

He dropped his handful of sample medical supplies on the tabletop. He rubbed his shin. "I fell over a box full of this stuff," he complained. "It was in the garage, a big box. Where did it come from?"

He had not known whether she would answer his tone, but this time she did, and she seemed flustered. Color came into her face, and she nervously straightened out the things he had deposited. "Leslie gave me these things," she said. "Oh, not all at once; she says they are samples the salesmen leave in the office. I've collected them to take to the church. For the clinic at Neighborhood House, you know?"

Yes, he did know. But — "Did you go to

the office?" he asked. She almost never did. Would Leslie have given her the things without expressing her surprise at Jan's appearance there?

"Did you go to the office?" he asked again.

"I phoned Leslie. I had been told — the women at the clinic said the other doctors gave them their samples . . ."

Yes. They did. Rather indiscriminately, Dick had always thought.

"She said it would be okay," Jan added.

He was still puzzled. His office did give away samples. Certain ones. And by other means.

"She didn't give you that big boxful; and why . . . ?"

"Oh, I've been collecting them. I had Jackson carry them out. He just dumped them inside your garage, I suppose."

"I suppose," Dick said dryly. "Go on back to bed. I was somewhat shaken by the near fall."

"I'm sorry."

Dick watched her turn and disappear around the turn in the stairs. What was strange? That she had told him as much as she had? That Leslie had been giving samples to Jan, and had not said one word to Dick? It was not like her to do such things.

Jan's head popped around the stair curve again. "If you find her doing other irregular things," she said brightly, "I could do her job."

Dick was shocked at the suggestion. Added to the other things he was puzzling about . . . "If you're talking about Leslie," he said flatly, "you could not do her job."

"You don't want me to."

"All right. I don't want you to. His office is no place for a doctor's wife. Any doctor, any wife!" His tone was rough, and he knew that Jan would be angered by it, that she was angered by the whole development.

She flared up hotly, coming to stand before him. "Look here, Dick Foster," she said. "You know I did secretarial work when you were interning. You know I could be a receptionist, and keep that sort of books! And I want that job! I *want* it. I am sick and tired of the place I have in your life — cooking, dusting, cleaning, being introduced as your wife, with no identity of my own."

"Oh, Jan, for heaven's sake, if you want to use your own name, go ahead. If you want a job outside of the home, get one!"

"You've been urging me to work."

"I know it. But never in my office. Find another doctor, or another line of work. The clinic at Neighborhood House could probably use you. For now, tonight, please let this house settle down so I can get some rest."

Did Jan put the article in the newspaper? Who told about the gremlins that moved flower beds and drew graffiti pictures? A day or two later, Dick went out for a consultation at the Veterans Hospital on a patient of his who was claiming disability pension, and returned to find the newspaper article on his desk and Jackson sitting in a chair in the waiting room. Dick only glanced at him.

He laid some official-looking papers before Leslie. "Perhaps you could come back to my office," he said.

"What'd they do to you out at the V.A.?" Jackson asked him. "They generally want someone they can blame things on if anything goes sour."

"Will you please clear out," Dick suggested coldly.

"I brung the newspaper . . ."

"It's on your desk, Doctor," said Leslie softly. "I've already said thank you."

Jackson got to his feet. "Then I might as well leave."

Leslie must have waited until he had departed. "What did he want?" Dick asked her, washing his hands. He reached for his white coat.

"He hangs around. Says he's learning things. He talks to the patients and their families."

"He hasn't any business here."

"I know that. But —"

"But he's hard to get rid of. Yes, I've discovered that. Leslie, do you give him drug samples?"

She looked up sharply from the papers she was arranging on his desk. "Then you did find some —"

"What are you talking about?"

She pointed to the newspaper clippings. "They say we have gremlins here."

Dick spread the clippings apart, read their gist swiftly, and faced Leslie, his expression blank. "Jackson?" he asked.

"I really don't think so."

Then it was Jan. Had he told her about the flower beds and the graffiti? No, there Jackson would have come in on the matter; he would have told her, at least.

Dick sat down in his chair, and ran his hand through his hair. "Will patients come or stay away from gremlins?" he asked, sounding tired. "And tell me. Did we use to run a fairly quiet, even dull, office around here? Before I became a docent, I mean."

She laughed. "Don't blame yourself."

"I don't. I blame the program. I never in the world would have known Jackson."

"Oh, yes, you would if you had begun to teach in the new medical school. You've also had the jump on Crans and Baus."

He nodded. "And I never bought a dozen peaches in my life but what one was brown around the seed."

"That's the spirit. Buzz when you're ready, Doctor."

"And if any detail men come in, ask them please not to leave any samples. I nearly mashed my pretty face when I fell over that box."

"That would have been a real shame," she said, laughing and leaving. But she was back almost at once. "Did he take that big box out of the storeroom?" she asked. "The *big* one?"

"I told you I nearly broke my neck."

"But, Dick, those weren't samples in that box. He may have added samples. Those were orders that came in yesterday, and I had not yet put them on the shelves."

"There were samples, too. That's what I scooped up and took into the house."

"But —"

"I brought the whole thing back; it's in the trunk of my car. Get someone, the custodian or maybe one of the tech girls, to help carry the thing in."

She laughed and went before him, out to the parking lot, where they lifted out the big box, set it on the blacktop, then carried it inside. "You've smeared your uniform," he told her.

"And your coat sleeves."

"I have other coats. Now, can we get these things into the cupboards, and locked up, before Jackson pays us another visit?"

"I'll work with the girls." She handed him his fresh coat. "Dick," she said unexpectedly. In the office she almost invariably called him "Doctor" or "Dr. Foster." But that morning, "Dick, does Mrs. Foster have a key to our office?"

He looked puzzled. "Why, she may, but I don't think so, Leslie. She never comes here."

"Well," Leslie stood uncertain. "The lab technician and the nurse have been missing things . . ."

"Drugs?" Dick asked sharply.

"No hard drugs. We keep them double-locked up. But antibiotics, equipment, like syringes, gloves, a speculum and dilator, some chemicals used in the lab. A few medicines. Darvon and such."

Dick stood shaking his head. "Oh, Lord!"

he breathed. What did he have on his hands?

Jan's story of the Neighborhood House would cover these missing things. Not all of them . . .

"What is going on?" asked Leslie.

Dick walked slowly down the hall. "I suppose, with the docent students coming in and out —"

They would have difficulty pinning anything on one person.

"Some," said Leslie dryly, "come in and out more than others."

"If we were talking to Kenny — or does he know these things?"

"He's missed things. A thermometer just a day or so ago."

"Well, if he were standing here with us, just about now he would mention my garage."

"Yes, he would, Doctor. So I'll do it for him."

"There has to be a connection," Dick admitted.

"Could you explain the problem to Janice — to Mrs. Foster?"

"No," said Dick. "Let's get to work."

But he remembered what had been said, and the brusque tone he had used to Leslie. So after hours — the afternoon had become rainy, and the patient list, with both doctors working, was covered by four o'clock — he called Kenny and Leslie to his office, quickly outlined to his partner what he and Leslie had discussed earlier. The big box of medical supplies in his garage — samples and pilferings from the office —

"All back where they belong," said Leslie quietly. "The box set out for the trash man, or for our visitor to see."

"Yes, and I snapped at Leslie," Dick confessed. "I'm sorry about that."

She shrugged. "As I've heard patients say, you were entitled."

"Not really. But I think I owe it to you two to tell you that there is developing — it began at the time of the first docent meeting, and has progressed rapidly since Christmas — but there definitely is a serious rift between Jan and me."

"It began with the docent meeting," said Kenny thoughtfully.

"What will you do?" asked Leslie.

Dick shook his head. "What I've been doing, probably," he admitted. "I married the woman. It was a mistake. I seem to be stuck with it."

He picked up his bag and went out. His two friends watched him go to his car.

"What *will* he do?" Leslie asked Kenny.

The doctor shook his head. "As he says, what he has been doing. A divorce, or even his moving out, would trigger such a row —"

"Living with that witch hurts his work, too, you know. Touches it, at least."

"Yes. He should have a peaceful life."

"I'd like to see him happy."

"He will be."

But before that could happen, before he could do anything about Jackson and the drug situation, Gene Foster decided to give a party.

Because of the rain that evening, Dick could not work in his garden. He decided to go across and talk to Gene for a time. "I may eat supper there," he told Jan.

"If invited."

"Even if I'm not. I'll tell the answering service."

"I'd send you word of any important call."

"I would hope so." He draped his raincoat over his head and struck down the drive and up the one to his brother's house. He liked a rainy summer evening — the colors freshened, the perfume from the flowers. The wooded hill behind their homes shimmered like green silk.

He stomped up on the stoop, hung his coat on a flower basket, and went inside.

"Anybody home?" he called, knowing that they were. Marlene called from the kitchen, and Gene came out from the family room.

"Well, if it isn't the doctor!" he said heartily. "Can you stay for supper?"

"I'd better. I told Jan I wouldn't be home." He took the phone and called the answering service, giving Gene's number.

As they ate Marlene's good dinner — red beans and ham cooked all day in the hot pot, a crisp salad, and fresh cookies with iced tea — Dick told Gene and Marlene about the stolen medical supplies, the "gremlins" in his office. He brought out the newspaper article and made a joke of the matter, not wanting Gene to become excited or angry.

He was concerned, certainly. "What are you going to do?" he asked.

"First, I wish Jackson were not black."

"Why?" asked Marlene. "You've treated him exactly the same as you have Reed Crans and the others."

"I've tried to do it that way. But it makes a difference. It should not, but it does. If I mark his report suggesting that he has certain character traits not suitable for medical training, there will be the biggest row made —"

"You've done it for others, haven't you?"

"Yes, but Jackson would make the row.

The newspapers, the equal righters would be on my back . . ."

"But, Dick, you were set to judge his fitness for medical training."

"I can only put down what I can prove he did. Does. How will it look? He finds ways of getting into my office after hours. He comes to my house when I am not there. It will read pretty foolishly."

"But he stole supplies and things called specula—" said Gene. "What in the devil *are* you going to do?"

Dick reached for another cookie. "Maybe I should just go and get good and drunk," he said. Then, to cover Marlene's protest, he added, "But I do hate the hangover. The waiting for the bedroom to sober up."

Gene laughed aloud.

"You never got that drunk," Marlene assured him confidently.

"What do you mean, I never did?" Dick demanded. "You can't get a good, firm M.D. without it. That's why women haven't any business studying medicine."

"Mrs. Baus isn't going to study here, is she?" asked Marlene, and for five minutes she and Dick discussed Alice Baus. They had come to like her. But Reed Crans was the best.

"Well, he had a lot going for him to begin with," Dick pointed out. "You must remember that. He does."

"Just as Jackson uses his advantages," drawled Gene. "And Jan — I think she knows exactly what she is doing. Encouraging the rascal, having him around — that all exerts further pressure on you, bud."

Dick nodded. "If I let it. Yes, it does."

"Well?"

"Then I'll just have to lean a little farther backward . . ."

"How far is that?" Gene kept his eyes sternly on his brother's face.

Dick sipped his iced tea. "Well, let's see what she wants. Lately, it's been Leslie's job at the office."

"She couldn't do that!" said Marlene scornfully.

"Does she still want you to move to the country?" asked Gene.

"She hasn't mentioned it recently. But it could be what she is working toward. She is persistent."

Gene pushed his chair back from the table. "There's one thing to remember, buddy-boy," he said. "Your profession will stand by you when your wife won't."

"Well, I like that!" protested *his* wife.

"I'm an exception, and you are too," Gene assured her, going around the table to pat her plump shoulder.

Chapter 7

It took arranging for the Gene Fosters to entertain. Marlene must speak to Dick about it; she must persuade Gene to have the dinner catered. "Just bring the food in, all ready to serve. I'll get some of the girls to set the table." That meant getting down the good china and crystal. "They'll come back and clear away if you don't want them at the dinner."

"I do," he said. "The whole adult family."

"I have something to talk about," he reminded her. "That's why I don't want you worn to a frazzle, or jumping up and down during the meal." Evidently he had adopted the catering idea as his own.

"I understand," she said quietly. "Don't get yourself excited telling me about it. We could go to a restaurant . . ."

"This is a family thing."

"Yes, dear. Of course it is."

So they planned the meal and invited the guests. Gene made a thing of crossing the lawn and inviting Dick and Jan. "It's a very special occasion," he said.

"And we'll be glad to come," Dick answered as gravely as if he had not heard of the affair before.

Jan said nothing, but after Gene had left she told Dick that, of course, she would not go.

"Then you should have told Gene so."

"You can tell him. It's almost a week away."

It was. "Why aren't you going?" Dick asked idly. It was intriguing, the excuses Jan thought up. She scarcely ever went anywhere socially.

"Lindsay and Leona will be there," said Jan, as if that would explain anything.

"But why shouldn't they be?" He was truly surprised. This was a new angle. "Don't you like them?"

Jan shrugged. "It doesn't make any difference how I feel about them. Lindsay is all right, I guess, and I scarcely know Leona. But I will say that Gene and Marlene are hypocrites."

"Oh, come on, Jan!"

"They are. Marlene cannot stand Leona. I've heard her say so. You know Gene didn't want Lindsay to marry her."

"Because they were too young. I don't think he dislikes her. He doesn't seem to."

"Yes! They both pretend."

Dick took a deep breath. "That is called getting along with people, Jan. You could practice and learn a little of it."

"I have no wish to learn and practice hypocrisy. I am sure Gene and Marlene feel awful about that child of theirs."

Dick said nothing. They all "felt awful."

"She isn't right, you know," Jan persisted.

No, she was not. It was a very sad thing in the family. The child would not live, which was a blessing. But Dick would not discuss the matter with Jan.

And he went to the dinner party. Making threats to Kenny and Leslie if he should be disturbed.

"Is this a black tie dinner?" Leslie asked.

"Oh, no. But I'll wear a suit and vest."

"My, my."

Dick departed, grinning.

The whole family had recognized the importance of the affair. The house was shining-pretty. A large cut-glass bowl of Dick's roses centered the table set with the best china and silver. The food was good. "I don't know when I've eaten capon," said Gene.

"Last winter," his wife reminded him. "I always get one at Christmastime and keep it in the freezer. Not this one, of course."

"And you don't stuff mushrooms, either,"

a niece pointed out.

When dessert had been served, and the waiters withdrew to the kitchen, Gene stood up, cleared his throat, and said that he had something to say.

"A speech?" asked a teen-ager in alarm.

"Yes, and a good one," Gene told him. And he made his little speech, which was a surprise to everyone but Marlene. Dick watched him carefully as he talked; he knew his brother was happy, but he must not get excited. He didn't. Not too excited. His cheeks flushed, and his eyes were bright as he announced that he would be brief. He only wanted to say that he was giving Lindsay — he looked across the table to where Lindsay sat, his bright hair shining in the light from the candles — he was giving Lindsay a block of stock in the Foster Machinery Company, with more to come each year. There was a rising buzz of talk and excitement. Gene held up his hand. "In my will," he said, "which I don't plan to have executed too soon, Lindsay will inherit the whole business. Marlene, my wife, has already been provided for."

It was a happy time. Lindsay was pleased — everyone was pleased. The young man would carry on as Gene had done. Dick took pictures of Lindsay, of Lindsay and

Leona and Kelly, their little girl. Regina — the other child — was in the hospital. These pictures could be used for the plant and news announcements. Marlene saw to it that the guests departed early. Gene was tired, whether he knew it or not. Dick sat on the couch beside him, showing him the pictures. "You have a family," he told his brother. "A son and a grandchild. I am envious."

Gene patted his arm. "Don't be. You have time to do something about a family, and have your own grandchild."

On the day after the party, Leslie talked to Kenneth about Dick's "gremlins." He would have full charge of the office that afternoon. "I think our friend Jackson is bugging him," she concluded.

"Why?"

Leslie frowned. "You don't think it is Jackson?"

"I don't know, but offhand I would say he had help, or at least direction."

Leslie went back to her desk and thought about the matter between receiving patients and sending them back to Kenny. Mrs. Parks wouldn't go. She would, she said, wait for the doctor. She meant Dick.

"He won't be here today," said Leslie.

"Well, where in the world is he?"

"Doctors have lives of their own, you know. Business, interests . . ."

"Girl friends," said a grumpy man who was in pain.

Leslie nodded.

"But Dr. Foster is married!" said someone else, her tone shocked.

"Couldn't he and his wife be off on a little romantic trip?" asked Mrs. Parks, switching her line of thought as she was so agile in doing. "Oh, the Doctor should be having children! He's sweet and kind, but not getting younger, is he, Miss Jackson?"

"No," said Leslie firmly. "Will you see Dr. Harrington, Mrs. Parks?"

The old lady rose and shook down her skirts, her coat and scarves; she collected her purse and her gloves. "I'll come back tomorrow," she announced. "Dr. Foster understands about my cancer."

"As you wish," said Leslie, drawing a line through the name on her appointment sheet. Not that Mrs. Parks made appointments; she just came in.

Over a cup of coffee midafternoon, Leslie told Kenny about Mrs. Parks.

"The old lady's right about one thing," said the young doctor. "Dick wants and should have children."

"With Jan?"

"No chance there, I'd say. Can't he get rid of her, Leslie?"

"She'd fight like a wildcat. Though I am sure he thinks about it."

"Where is he this afternoon?"

"Out in the hills. You've heard him speak of Dr. Mayhack?"

"Oh, yes. The doctor who started him in medicine. Retired now —"

"Yes, and not at all well. When he retired, he built a small house for himself and his wife out on a bluff overlooking the river, and they have enjoyed the place. But now — well, that's where Dick went this afternoon. I think the gremlin bit had got on his nerves — or his temper, rather. He is trying to decide what to do about Jackson."

"And maybe himself. His own life."

Leslie set her cup down and answered the telephone.

If peace and serenity would do it, Dick should find some help that afternoon. It was a warm day, but with a good breeze blowing. At Dr. Mayhack's home he found the comfort of old friends, the sorrow of their imminent loss. Both doctors knew this, and talked of the river, the fishing, the apples which were beginning to turn color on a tree down by the gate.

"It was good of you to come, Dick," said the host when Dick was ready to leave. "I know you are busy."

"I have a first-class partner."

"You're lucky. Come again."

"I shall. And you —"

"I'll call you if we need anything."

Dick waved his hand to the old people on the porch, and drove away, thinking of many things. The road he must travel to reach the highway was steep, and there were curves. He must watch for a dozen things, even a young deer who stood gazing at him. Dick stopped his car until the animal strolled off into the woods. As he waited, he spotted the stones of an old cemetery. A churchyard? More likely a family burying plot, with the house long gone. The headstones were small, hand-graven, many of them toppled. And yet —

Dick pulled his car off the road, got out, and started through the underbrush, raspberry vines snagging at his light trousers. There were a dozen graves in the small clearing. Dick was sure he had not visited this place before, but it held the same peace as did the burial ground he had once seen at Old Mystic — the quiet, the sureness. He bent over to straighten one of the fallen stones, and crouched there, frowning. Was this a case of *déja vu?* Or *had* he seen this place before, this stone? He took out his pocket knife and scraped at the lettering.

"Infant daughter." And the name — the family name? — of Hassen or Haussen. And the year. 1870. December.

But what really held his attention was the medallion above the name. An oval, faced with cloudy glass, and under it the countenance of a child. A baby. Yes! Infant Haussen. In the old days, in Italy today, in Italian-American cemeteries, he had seen photographs of the dead thus displayed. This was such a photograph, old, faded, the medallion was a little loose.

The photograph was that of a wizened baby with clenched fists, and eyes that were amazed at nothing. And on the stone were graven lines — words. With his knife he scraped dust from the grooves. And he read the words aloud as he discovered each one.

The baby sleeps in the graveyard
Roses in her ears
Cloves in her tiny fingers
Lavender in the blanket that wraps her.
Birds sing in the trees,
Rain washes the grave . . .

A further line he could not decipher.

As he knelt, puzzled, he heard a sound. A step? He rose, looked about. And saw nothing. A dog perhaps, or a raccoon.

He shrugged and reached into his pocket, took out his appointment book, and on a blank page he sketched the tombstone, the medallion. He spanned it with his fingers, and wrote down the dimensions in his careful, almost cryptographic script. Then he took off his jacket, and with a stick he scraped enough dirt away to set the small tombstone upright, the face again in place. He went to his car, wiped his hands on a rag from the glove compartment, put on his jacket, and started again for home, looking back as he drove slowly away. The little burial ground had melted almost into the underbrush and low-hanging tree leaves. He did not know why he had been so "taken" by that child's pictured face. Perhaps Gene's talk of a family, a grandchild . . .

The thought of it stayed with him as he checked his hospital patients, went to the office and read the lists of patients and phone calls which Leslie had left on his desk. He carefully locked the doors and went across the street to Research. Sister sat at the admissions desk, and he took the chair facing her. She smiled. "Tired," she decided.

"Not really," said Dick. "I took most of the afternoon off to see Dr. Mayhack."

Sister's eyes lifted, and Dick shook his head.

"It's too bad."

"I have decided it is harder when one knows the facts in a case."

"God will be merciful to that good man."

"I hope so."

"So many things seem to be too bad lately," he said slowly. "I don't usually dwell on these matters."

"You need a good game of tennis or sandlot baseball," she said briskly.

Dick laughed. He had played such baseball with Sister herself when he had been an intern and she in charge of the nurses' training school. Her skirts tied up, her arms swinging. "Were those our happy days?" he asked curiously.

"Oh, no. Life goes along, small hummocks, mountains, deep valleys. You've let yourself get stuck in a deep valley this spring and summer."

"My fault?"

"If you let it be."

He thought that over. He would not speak of Jan, or Jackson, or his brother's providing for his death. Sister knew all about those valleys. He looked up. "I came across something today," he said, and he told her about the old burial lot, the fallen stone, and the baby's picture, the poem.

"As if it were almost alive," he said, "or embalmed there."

"No," said Sister calmly. "No. But I have seen some startling things. I used to think such memorials were morbid. *Sick* is the modern word. They are not, necessarily. Let me tell you about something that happened here, Doctor. In this hospital. Just a minute —"

She answered the beeping telephone, and turned back to Dick. "When we first occupied this building," she said, "we had a girl training to be a pathologist's assistant. She was assigned here — our pathologist was getting along in years — and she didn't find enough work to keep busy. She helped the doctor, and learned to photograph tissue and things of that sort. She also was the one to photograph the babies born on Maternity.

"Now, some years before, she had visited her grandfather's farm, and had found the family cemetery. Maybe the same one you came across today. A little face embedded in stone fascinated this girl. And when a baby died, she would make a replica tombstone of heavy cardboard or Styrofoam, and insert the baby's picture in it. It was a harmless thing to do, I thought, but it upset some people and we had to stop it."

"Where did she do this?"

"She had a darkroom up on the top floor. She went beyond the picture taking, I'm afraid. In small quantities, she brought in dirt — she used empty paint buckets, I believe. And she re-created a small grave which she decorated — set up the Styrofoam headstone with the baby's picture —" Sister glanced back at Dick. "As I say, it revolted some people. So we transferred the girl elsewhere, and gave the pathologist strict orders."

"And cleaned the supply room."

"Why the whole floor is supposed to be cleaned regularly."

"What did you do with the pictures?"

Sister looked shocked, then thoughtful. She looked at her watch; she looked up at the clock. She spoke into the phone and asked someone to take the desk for half an hour. Then she came out into the hall with Dick.

"I suppose there were records," she said as they walked to the elevator, the tall, strong man, the dumpling of a woman with her full skirts, white apron, and bobbing coronet. No modern habits for Sister Alphonsus!

"Didn't people get curious about your girl and her buckets of dirt?" he asked as they entered the elevator.

"I suppose they did, and she would say, 'Don't ask!' "

Dick laughed. "And so many crazy things go on in a hospital, they probably didn't ask."

"That's right. Here, push this button, and we go to the top."

"Spooky," said Dick.

There was light from the street illumination, the last glow from the sun, the lighted upper floors of the office building across the street. But, yes, it was spooky. Dick took his pen-light from his pocket, and guided Sister's feet. "Spooky enough," he said, "with memorialized babies."

He turned the knob of the door marked Central Supply, and they went in. The shelves were empty, a cupboard door swung open to nothingness. But in a far corner, beyond the worktable —

"Good Lord!" said Dick, below his breath. "That's reverent, Sister."

She crossed herself. "I think so, too," she said. "We need more light . . ."

He turned the small beam across the windows — he had seen just such a light up here — and focussed it on the corner. And there it was, a tombstone such as he had seen that afternoon and had set straight. A mounded heap of dirt, and flowers — faded and dry — but surely they had come from the motel's beds. And an oval carved in the face of the small white "stone." On the table was an oval of the same size. He picked it up in his hand. Faced with convex glass, it was the little doll-house mirror frame which his knife had whittled and shaped before Christmas.

Sister was talking about family rights. "We tried to keep this quiet," she said breathlessly.

She had from Dick. But not from Jan.

Dick picked up the frame, and the newspaper clipping which lay near it. He touched Sister's arm. "Let's go downstairs before the battery wears out," he said, guiding her to the hall where the light was better, to the elevator.

Downstairs he took her to the coffee shop, and bought coffee for both of them. "Food?" he asked.

She shook her head. "I shouldn't lose control," she said. "This was coincidence."

That Dick, on the same day, had found the little cemetery. Yes, that was coincidence. Had someone followed Dick that afternoon? Expecting to find something more incriminating than a visit to a sick friend? Jan, or Jackson, would be capable of doing such a thing. Knowing that Dick was capable of not "seeing" even Jan's car. He laid the small mirror on the Formica table top. Sister looked at him questioningly.

"I made that," he said. "It's much smaller, of course, than the one in the cemetery. Someone stole it. Someone found out about the little graveyard upstairs."

"I should have checked," said Sister, still visibly distressed.

"You have a housekeeper. But you're right. We both should check our surroundings. Now if you'll allow me to clean the stuff out of the supply room . . ."

"Do you know who — ?"

"I think I do. And if not, my efforts to throw things out should bring the monster to the surface. You might concentrate on tighter security for those two top floors. Of course, after I get safely out . . ."

This brought a faint smile to Sister's face.

Dick nodded. Well, for one thing, he had to make up his mind what to say in his report on Jackson! "I have to check on the office," he said, "and get home."

Sister rose. "Thank you, Doctor . . ." she said uncertainly. "It's good to have you around."

* * *

Kenneth Harrington saw him drive from the parking lot. Now what had Dick wanted at the office? Of course there could be a dozen things, but Kenny had not thought he would be back.

He went inside and checked the answering service, attended to one call from a pharmacist about refilling a prescription, and went on to his own office for the record he needed. He opened the folder, spread the papers on his desk, and made note of the medicines this particular patient was now taking. He lifted his head. Had he heard a door hinge creak? Snapping switches, he went into the hall, looked both ways, and saw a shadow gliding out through the parking lot door. "Hey!" he shouted. "Wait up!"

The presence of the security guard twenty feet away made the man do just that. He even sauntered a step toward Dr. Harrington's car.

"What were you doing in the office?" Kenny asked him.

"It ain't late, Doc."

"It is after eight — almost nine o'clock. And you have no reason to be here in broad daylight."

"Dick — Dr. Foster, you know — he lets

me use the lab sometimes."

"I don't think that's true, Jackson."

"Yes, 'tis, Doc. You could call him. But right here —" he tugged at his right hip pocket and produced a flat, black-bound book. "See? I keep a record o' cases I work on."

"What sort of work do you do?" asked Kenny scornfully. He was wondering if he was strong enough to handle Jackson if the man got ugly. He flipped through the book. They were patients' records, done in the code which the office used. "Dr. Foster will give this back to you," he decided, putting the book down into the pocket of his light jacket.

"Aw, Doc, don' be that way."

"I know the way I am and should be. I am not at all certain about you, Jackson. Do you have a key to our office?"

"Not to keep. I give it back to Mrs. Foster."

"Why does she lend it to you?" Kenny had not known that Jan had a key. "Your work with us is over, you know."

"I keep learnin'. And Miz Foster, she's int'rested."

"Well, let me have the key. I'll see that she gets it back." He held out his hand. "Unless Dr. Foster says you need to have one —"

"He's a busy man. He can't be bothered. Jus' this afternoon he had a ruptured appendix and a kid hit on the head with a baseball."

Kenny knew where Dick had been. He still held out his hand for the key and Jackson, reluctantly, dropped it into his palm. "Whut I gonna tell Jan?" he asked.

"Tell her you are sorry you called her by her first name," said Kenny, going on to his car. As he drove out, he would speak to the security guard, though by that time Jackson would be long gone. Still —

Should Kenny tell Dick what had happened? The man had enough on his mind. Perhaps he should talk to Janice. Oh, no! He would not ever do that! He would not even give her the key. He feared and disliked the woman. Perhaps he would give the key to Dick, or leave it with Leslie . . . Maybe Jackson would tell Jan that Kenny had confiscated her key, and she would make a row. All right! He could handle that. But he did not think it would be mentioned. And Dick was busy enough . . .

Dick was busy. He was on the staff of three hospitals; he made those rounds every morning. He attended consultations with the specialists he used on referrals, his mind alert, his interest keen. He saw patients, old and new, in his office five afternoons, and part of some mornings, of each week. Always he was subject to interruption. "Doctor, will you sign this, please?" "Doctor, you are wanted on the house phone." "Doctor, there is a patient of yours down in emergency —" He must keep himself physically fit, and his mind strictly on the patient under consideration. A primary doctor needed to know a lot of medicine, to keep up on the best and latest techniques and treatments. And above all, he must listen to and heed his own favorite lecture to students and doctors in training.

"The purpose of medicine is to insure health. Make that *your* prime purpose."

Now that they had the beginning of a medical school in their city, he must do his quota of lecturing, training, and explaining.

He was popular. He liked people, and they liked him. They spoke to him, they detained him — "Oh, Doctor!" Perhaps it was to speak of some professional matter, more often — "My Irish setter had six pups. They are beauties. If you want one —"

He was asked to take trips. "You have the right ideas, and get positive about them —"

But Dick had little time or taste for big

medical convocations. Yes, he would learn. Yes, he did think the A.M.A. should insist on a national standard of medical performance. How could every doctor be trusted to judge himself or others? If there were a standard —

Now that they were into the medical training bit, they must not let their students, once they got their licenses, decide that nothing further was required of a doctor.

This he stated at a staff meeting about the performance of one man. As a docent, his opinion was desirable, he was told. He said wisdom was desirable, but being a docent had taught him how little he knew.

"Weren't you chosen docent because of your wisdom, your knowledge?"

Dick laughed. "If I was the best you could find, you're in trouble."

"Would you take it on again?"

Dick clasped his hands over his ears. "Never, never, never!" he declared.

"Why not?"

He sat thoughtful. "Well, because I am uncertain of my own performance many times. How can you teach if you yourself do not know?"

"You're an excellent doctor, Dick."

"How do you know? How do I know? A patient gets well, but another one does not.

How can one judge?"

They talked on, and he went to answer a telephone call. He did not return to the meeting. All day he had been thinking of what should he do about Jackson? It seemed impossible to persuade him that the way of work, books, study was the best way, the sure way.

"Dr. Foster!" It was the girl at the desk. "Will you call your office?"

He glanced at his watch. Glory be, he was late! But — He picked up the phone, pushed buttons, he talked to Leslie. "I am not trying to say I'm sorry," he told her. "I'll be there as soon as traffic allows. What? Yes, I am all right. And I remembered two minutes ago that it was Harrington's afternoon off. Bye, sugar. I'll be there."

He punched himself out of the hospital, stopping for a minute to tell himself that he was at Children's, and he descended to the parking lot level; his car stood out in the bright sunlight. There were leaves blowing about in a stiff breeze. Some of the leaves were red-yellow. Sweet gums turned early. They were handsome trees, but they did litter one's lawn. He came to a full stop. For there was a girl, a young woman, though she had the clear inquiring eyes of a young girl, even a child. Her hair was thick and taffy-gold, cut earlobe length, combed thickly and smoothly. She was leaning against the hood of a small foreign car. She glanced at Dick as he approached, and smiled when he said, "Hi!" as he did to almost everyone. Anyone. He took a second, closer look at the girl. She was, he thought, what he would call a wholesome young woman. She was wearing a fluffy pink sweater over well-fitted but comfortable white slacks. He came back a few steps. "Well, hello!" he said warmly.

She laughed. Softly. "Good morning, Doctor," she said; there was the hint of an accent. The way she spoke the last syllable of "Doc-tor." Not British. He liked her thick, fair hair, her clear skin, and especially her lovely eyes.

"Do you know me?" he asked.

"Certainly. I have worked here in this hospital all this past year."

And he had not seen her before. "Then I should know you," he said.

This time her laughter came freely, not loud, more like the soft ripple of one's hand lightly across the treble keys of a piano. The song of water running swiftly over stone. "You do know me," she said. "You speak to me."

"Oh, I speak to just about everybody. But

I am sure I never *saw* you before."

"I am a Volunteer. I work all over the hospital."

"Are you having trouble with your car? A problem?"

"I seem to have a flat tire. I have been trying to decide what to do."

"You call a garage."

"Yes, but do I wait here, or call a taxicab, go home and then call? Is it safe to leave the keys? Do I tell them to deliver the car — where? Here? To my home?"

Dick pursed his lips and nodded. "You have a problem, all right," he agreed. "Let's see. There are various solutions. We can add my car to the picture and the fact that I think you are a very pretty girl."

"And you are a busy doctor."

There was that, and the promise to Leslie that he would not be very late. He did not mention those things. But between them they did decide that they would call the garage from the hospital desk, and leave the car keys. Service was promised within the hour.

"But you can't believe a thing they say! I tell you. We'll leave the key, I'll take you to lunch. No! Not here in the hospital! Then I can take you home, or bring you back here —"

"And you can return to your office," said the girl softly.

He sighed. "Yes, I have to do that! But —" His eyes brightened. "Not before we have lunch! I told my secretary that I would eat lunch."

Had he? No, he didn't think so.

"Aren't you busy, Doctor?"

"Of course. But after your working here a year, don't you agree it is time I got to know you? There is a restaurant close by —" He spoke earnestly to the girl at the desk. His new friend's name was Heidi Marie Kreuger — that explained the accent — and there was a restaurant. In the close-by shopping center, a feature of an elegant shop. There they could, and did, order quiche, and they talked. Miss Kreuger already knew that he was a staff doctor. Dr. Foster, yes. And the children liked him, but not always the medicines he prescribed.

"Well, they go and catch heavy coughs — you can't cure the things without nasty, sticky-sweet cough medicine! My goodness, look at that!"

That was a model, showing a chiffon party dress. She was tall, willowy —

"I don't think she wears much under it," said Dick's companion.

"I don't think she wears a rag!" He smiled

at the model. "We won't buy that one," he said in his friendly way. He turned back to his guest. "Now, tell me all about yourself."

She looked startled, then she laughed. Her soft, pretty laughter. "You know my name. I come from Austria, high up in the Alps. I came here as an exchange student. I was here but two months when my father had a stroke and I must return home. This broke my heart. But my family here, the ones to whom I was assigned, they arranged, after my father recovered enough — he is still somewhat paralyzed, but he can write, he is a professor — they arranged for me to return, stay with them, and study. They are very kind. I also do the hospital work, which I like. One young man in my family — the family that took me in — he is going to study medicine, and —"

Dick leaned forward. "Reed Crans?" he asked.

She smiled and nodded. "You see? I know all about you, Dr. Foster. You are his great hero."

Then why — He spoke the question aloud. "Why, with you in his family for a year, is he running after one of the Tabler girls?"

"Because he is in love." She watched his face.

Dick nodded. "Yes, I think he is. Has he talked about me?"

"About the fine doctor you are, how much he has learned from you. He says you have a beautiful home, and raise roses. You also make doll houses and doll furniture."

Had Crans talked about Jan? Did Heidi Marie know that Dick was a man unhappy in his marriage so unhappy, so bent on contemplating that unhappiness that he forgot there were girls like this, pretty, intelligent, desirable . . .

He gave himself a mental shake. She was talking about her home in Austria. Her father had wanted her to come to America, and to stay if that was what she wanted to do.

"Is it?" asked Dick intently.

Her cheeks turned a rosy pink. "Now it is," she said shyly.

She reminded him of his office duties, and they went back to the hospital; her tire had been replaced, and he had no further reasons to delay. But he would see her again, and she knew that he would.

Driving to the office, he thought back over the last hour. This girl — he saw and met girls, pretty young women, often. But this one — she was not a patient. With her there was not the tension which emanated from Janice. Certainly she was not Leslie, the warmly willing woman, good at her job, better in other things. Occasionally Dick had thought that if Jan, who knew about Leslie and sometimes made acid remarks about her, had taken time to study Leslie, the "other woman" she called her — if Jan had realized that Leslie was what Dick wished his wife might be, well-groomed, thoughtful of him, ready to listen to him talk of his interests, and to express her love for him — things would have been entirely different in the Foster home.

Well, they were going to be different now! He could, he thought, feel sure that Crans would have spoken of how things were between Dick and his wife. So now he could do what was necessary —

He wanted Heidi Marie. Every nerve in his body wanted her. He remembered that when he was about eighteen, and Gene older, of course, and their mother had died, his father had said of his wife, "I loved her, I liked her. I was never angry with her. There had not been a single minute when I did not love her."

With this new girl, he thought —

Would such pleasure and comfort ever be given to Dick? Oh, it could be! It would be. They would be together. He would stroke that thick, soft hair, kiss those pretty lips; they would make love, of course, but there were more things that he had learned to want from a woman. He wanted to be with Heidi, to *be* with her. He wanted all the little things, to sit together, their fingers intertwined, and listen to the wrens who built their nests above one of the house doors, and sang, and sang! To walk with her in the dusk of evening, to wake beside her at dawn. He wanted to *love,* and be loved. He needed that, he must have it! But how was he to get those things?

Could he tell Jan that he had found a woman he wanted to marry, and ask her . . . ? He would give her everything he had! It had not been enough when there had been no other woman. What would she say and do? What would *he* do? But he was sure that there would be a way. He would see Heidi again and again, he would offer his love, his name — and he would *do* something!

He was whistling when he came into the office. Yes, he knew that he was late. Who was the first patient?

The nurse and Leslie looked at each other. "What's happened to *him?*" asked the nurse.

Leslie laughed and shook her head. "Ten years ago, I would have said he was in love."

"He's not old."

"He's not old at all. But there is Mrs. Foster."

"Yeah," said the nurse. "Yeah, there sure is."

When Kenny came back to the office at four-thirty, Leslie found a minute to speak of Dick and his euphoria. "It won't do him any good to be in love, will it?" she asked.

"It might," said Kenny. "Because if it's really love, old Dick is going to do something about it."

He glanced at Leslie. "All right with you?"

"Of course it's all right. I want that guy to have some sort of life."

Dick wanted it, too. Achingly. That very evening, he would have gone to the Crans home; but he did not go. He could not.

For three days he hoped to see Heidi again at Children's Hospital, but he did not. Then he had an inspiration. He might have to go to jail to contact her again, but it would be worth it.

He went to see Crans that third evening, the first time he had been in the tall town house where Reed lived with his parents, his sister, and Heidi Marie.

He reminded Reed of the syphilophobia case which had reached a crisis during the time that Dick was docent for Crans. Dr. Foster had changed the lab report to positive and had been giving the woman a placebo. Reed smiled. He remembered.

"Yes!" said Dick. He watched the doorway that showed the hall and stairs. "One day last week that patient's sister, who often came with her, took the report from my desk. I was called to another room. And now I have been haled into court on a charge of forgery. The hearing is tomorrow."

"And I may go?"

"I thought you would be interested."

"I am. Of course I am. What time?"

"Two o'clock. There's to be a jury, my lawyer insisted on that, in the County Court. I'll look for you." He stood up as if to leave. "I met your exchange student," he said, blurting the announcement as he would have done at fifteen.

"Heidi told me. She was very taken with you. She said you had been very kind."

"Do you think she might want to come to my trial with you?"

Reed laughed. "You're sure of being acquitted?"

"I am. I have an array of doctors as witnesses. In any case, I want to see Heidi again."

"Doctor . . ."

"I know. I have a wife."

"She knows that, too. Last winter when I

stayed in your home, I am afraid I told my family, at dinner one evening, that I had been living in a home where a wife actually was only cook and housekeeper and seemed to like it. I said I felt sorry for you. Heidi remembers that. She said that you were much younger than she had pictured you when I told about your home. She said she wished you were not married at all."

"And she knows that I must do something about it before —"

"She will be friends, but it is our duty —"

"I'll set things straight."

"How?"

"I don't know. But there will be a way. I'll talk to my lawyers."

"Tomorrow you had better stick to the syphilis case."

Dick laughed. "I'd better, hadn't I? But you'll bring Heidi?"

"We'll be there."

The trial took place, and Heidi, in a white blouse and blue suit, leaned forward eagerly to hear the testimony of Dr. Foster. He had secured the testimony of several doctors, well known in the city. And the jury acquitted the accused, their decision being that a physician was entitled to give false information for the patient's own good.

Afterward, Reed tactfully had a class, and

Heidi said, yes, she would drive home with Dr. Foster. "My name is Dick," he told her. "I am ten years older than you are, and I am sure I have fallen in love with you."

"But —"

"That will be arranged. It may take a little time, but we can see each other —"

Chapter 8

And they did see each other. Not speaking of Dick's love, Heidi acknowledging her pleasure in him only by the color in her cheeks and the brightness of her eyes.

On her days at Children's Hospital, Dick saw her as often as could be managed. They talked together. Over lunch at the cafeteria, driving home in her car, or his, going back by cab for the abandoned one; once arranging to have someone drive Dick's car to his office, once bringing Heidi back and making the transfer openly, laughing. Dick telling her to inform the interested watchers that they had been to a cemetery.

They had been. They had sat long on the dried grass, holding hands, watching a Bewick wren, wondering why the common wren was called jenny. Dick told of the one which, each spring, built a nest over the side door of his home.

"They gather the darnedest collection of sticks and dead grass and shreds of paper. One spring Jan attempted to brush them down. After she had destroyed several nests, I told her to stop."

"Did she?"

"Oh, yes. In things like that, she does as I say. I like the wrens. When they have fledglings, the male works like the devil to bring food to the nest. And he sings to split your ears. I used to think he was a model of husbandry fidelity, but after watching him for a whole Sunday, I decided that he sang from several locations because he was scouting an area and helping a second female build a nest."

"Should I be shocked?" asked Heidi, laughing.

"I was not. His first wife — all female wrens are great fussers. The males sing, the females fuss."

It was harmless talk between a man and a young woman. Anyone might have listened. But for Dick and Heidi there were so many hidden meanings, the casual brush of her elbow against his sleeve, the quick glances between them. They knew, they waited. To be together was enough. For now.

After the first trip to the old cemetery, Heidi asked if they might go again.

"It will be cold and windy on that hill above the river."

"This won't take long. But, reading in father Crans's library the other night, I found something. It isn't about babies, but — I want you to read it there."

"Then we shall go."

And they did. On the sunny, windy Saturday before Thanksgiving. And Heidi brought out the sheet of paper on which she had painstakingly copied the page which had struck her.

The remains of Kirklees Priory stand next to a pub called "The Three Nuns."

There is a stone on the grave:

> Here underneath dis laitl stean
> Laz robert earl of Huntington
> He'er arcir ver as hie sa geud
> An pipl kauld im robin heud
> Sick utlawz as hi an is men
> Vil england niver si agent

Dick read it. He read it again, and tucked the paper into his pocket. Then he turned to Heidi, and for the first time he kissed her. She clung to him fiercely, then drew away.

"We must not," she said breathlessly.

"We must!" And both knew that they would.

Perhaps the Crans family guessed the change in the relationship. At any rate, when plans were being made for Thanksgiving, they did not invite Dr. Foster.

Jan said she would roast a turkey if Dick wanted to invite Gene and Marlene. "But not all the kids."

"I've said I would do house duty at Children's that day."

"Is the Tabler baby . . . ?"

"She gets no better. Of course. I think Gene and Marlene are going to one of the Tabler homes; they've asked me, and would ask you —"

"I'll do house duty myself," said Jan tartly, turning away.

At the hospital there were papier-mâché turkeys on the patients' trays. Turkey to eat, pumpkin pie — and two accident cases to keep Dick and the E.R. resident busy. Dick took the occasion to examine Lindsay's older daughter, a brain-damaged child, born brain-damaged, with no chance ever to grow, to see, or speak. Leona had wanted to care for her. But Dick stopped that. Leona was not trained. There could be, and was, another child in the home, healthy, happy, normal. The little morsel of humanity in the crib at the hospital did not know where she was, who she was. Life hung by a thread, her heart and lungs and brain constantly monitored . . .

Still, Leona came to the hospital almost every day; Lindsay did often. Grieved, concerned, good people.

The Tabler family was so large that about twenty people sat down to dinner that Thanksgiving. Marlene pointed out to Gene how Lindsay had acquired a position of importance since being made "just about head" of the Foster Company.

"I hoped he would be accorded respect. The man works hard, Marlene. And I trust him — that takes a load from me."

"Then it was a good move."

Dick was missed, and talked about. He was being Doctor of the Day at Children's — the term must be explained and commented on. Jan's name came up briefly. And someone said he had heard that the doctor had a girl friend.

"Hush such talk," Marlene admonished. "We don't want Jan catching on and making a move."

"Is he going to divorce her?"

"We won't talk about it."

Dick could imagine the scene, the table, the people, the food. The talk and laughter . . .

He tried to picture Heidi in that group.

She would fit right in, probably bake the hot rolls. She could cook, she assured him. And if her father did come to America, they would have a little apartment. Reed thought the University would employ them in some way. Foreign language librarian had been mentioned.

Dick told himself to be happy for Heidi, but he was jealous. He wanted her all for himself. He —

And then it happened.

Lindsay Tabler, alone in his car, having gone to the company's building and warehouses and yards to check after a holiday, was found at the side of a park road, slumped over the wheel of his car, dead.

Almost forty years old, a successful man — on the rise in his business.

"Had he a history of heart disease?" Dick was asked by the police, the coroner.

"I don't know. He was not a patient of mine."

Marlene reminded Gene that she had told him to have Lindsay get a checkup before handing over half of the business to him. Now Leona would marry again; she would claim the business —

Dick told her to be quiet, to take care of Gene. Yes, this was a tragic thing. He had been called at the hospital — the news had come back to the various homes —

"Does there have to be an inquest? An autopsy?" asked Gene.

"Don't let it disturb you. Grieve for Lindsay, but for now forget what comes later."

He was concerned for Gene because it was known that Gene did "have a heart." Yes, Dick promised his brother, and Leona, he could attend the autopsy. It would not be bad. They would look first at the heart.

And they found what Dick suspected — a ruptured aneurysm.

"Did he know . . . ?" Gene asked his brother.

"Two minutes before he died. Enough time to pull to the side of the road."

"What am I going to do without him?"

"Take care of yourself, first thing. So you will have time to make arrangements. For now, let yourself, let us all, grieve for a fine young man."

Everyone did grieve. Each member of the family, and each one, like Dick, was afraid that the shock would affect Gene. "The sooner we can get his business affairs in order," Dick told Marlene, he told Heidi, and others, "the better it will be for Gene."

The funeral was large. Lindsay and Gene Foster were prominent in the city's business circles. Marlene and a sister were keeping Kelly. "Children don't belong at funerals," said Leona. She came from the hospital where she had sat for an hour beside Regina's crib, weeping softly, asking herself, thought Dick, why it must be Lindsay, not this poor child. Dick and Gene took care of her at the services.

Jan did not attend.

"She could have," thought Dick angrily. "She could have!" And he sat in the pew, aware of Heidi's presence with the Crans family, and thought of the biography he had been reading of John Butler Yeats. "I married my first wife without being one bit in love with her." So the elder Yeats had done, so Dick Foster had done, and was now paying for the mistake, if not sin.

He held Marlene's hand warmly in his. She was grieving more than she should, but, indeed, as she said, she had told Gene not to sign so much stock to Lindsay. "If anything happened to him, Leona would get it. She could marry again and you would have a stranger running and owning —" He shook his head. Those things would be handled later.

Lawyers, Leona — Dick had his brother to worry about, his profession, and his plans for his own future.

The funeral was on Saturday. On Friday, Kenny had given Dick more than a backlog of patients with whom to concern himself. The day after a holiday, all the details of his family problems attendant on Lindsay's death.

"Do what you have to do," Kenneth told him. "But I do have something to show you."

"I have time if it is important. I'll keep in touch with Gene through Marlene. What's been happening here?"

"I'll show you. Then I'll do whatever you tell me to do."

"I confer with you, pardner, I don't pass out orders."

"In this case, I'd like some orders."

"I'm getting all of that I can handle in my own family these days."

Earlier, Kenny and Leslie had both expressed their sorrow at Lindsay's death.

"All right," Kenny said now. "Then I'll tell you. Leslie did the statistics."

Dick turned to look sharply at his "pardner."

"You started this investigation," said Kenneth, motioning to Dick to sit down at the desk. "Then you became somewhat diverted. Busy. Preoccupied. Now it's your brother's health. But —"

"How and when did I start this *thing* of

yours?" Dick demanded. "And speak up, son. My time —"

"I know. And we have patients waiting. Here and at the hospitals. Well, you started it by falling over a box of detail men's drug samples and some things filched from this office."

"Jackson?"

"Jackson. He's been laying in a nice bundle of supplies. Everything from Q-tips to instruments. He's had help."

"Not in this office!"

"In your home. Leslie and I have been keeping close count on things that come in here, and lately the things that go out unaccounted for. We've established a rule which we mean to clamp down on you that every Band-Aid used, every shot given —"

Dick was looking at the papers. He glanced up at Kenny. "Hard drugs?" he asked. "I remember the samples."

"If any hard drugs slipped through, it was the exception. Maybe some amphetamines, Darvons. Mainly the thievery has been medications such as we keep and administer here. No prescription drugs. But supplies — dressings, antiseptics, antibiotics, gloves — all sorts of supplies. Sterile dressings, pads, adhesive rolls . . ."

"How long have you been checking? I

know. Since I found that box. How long had the thievery . . . ?"

Kenny shrugged. "Since that time, we've checked our records, ingoing, outgoing. To get all the evidence, we have hidden here, after hours —"

"Leslie?" Dick spoke sharply.

"More often, I did it. We've trailed the fellow . . ."

"Jackson."

"Yes, of course. And do you know, my trusting, troubled friend, that the man had set up his own office. He calls it a health center. He uses what you've taught him —"

"He's smart."

"Yes, and he's got a lot of supplies. He is in and out of here a lot."

Dick groaned. "I thought he was just an eager beaver. Have you looked over at the hospital?"

"We've alerted Sister. But you — we're going to show you. It's Saturday and usually — Can you come out to my house about five this evening?"

"Oh, I don't know, Kenny. Marlene and Gene need me."

"It isn't a good time. But we think this is crucial."

"You mean the Jackson Health Center is about —"

"Yes, I do. And we can bring the police in. We mean to. But we wanted you to see —"

Dick said that he would meet him. "Now let's get a little work done here."

He worked hard all that day, and kept track of Gene. "Don't let him talk to a lot of people," he advised Marlene.

"Leona is not having a visitation."

"Good! I never did believe in wakes."

At five, he was ready for Dr. Harrington. "You won't like any of this, boss," he was warned. "We'll use my wife's car."

Jackson might not recognize it so readily. But the first place they drove to was the street where Dick himself lived, and past his house. "It's become routine," said Kenny. "I told you we had been trailing the man."

Dick could say little. There were three cars at Gene's house. One of them Reed Crans's. Heidi Marie might be with him. Kenny braked abruptly, and Dick looked at him in protest.

"Coming up from the bus stop," said Kenny, speaking softly as if the tall man in red slacks and plaid shirt, a loose jacket, might hear him. Their car would seem to be one of those before the Gene Foster home, but the tall man was going to the side door of Dick's house, and Jan appeared to be expecting him. She opened the door, stepped out on the stoop, and handed the man — Jackson — something that glinted under the light.

"She's giving him the office key," said Kenny.

"You told me you had taken it away from him."

"His key, not Jan's."

"How does she happen to have one?"

"She has one. I took the first one away from him; she must have had another made. If he had been as smart as he thinks he is, he would have had a duplicate made for himself."

"But how does all that go on?"

"They start with yours. Maybe only the front door key, maybe the others on your ring. When you go to bed, you probably drop your keys on the hall table. I do, to be sure I take them when I leave in the morning, or get called."

"I do that, yes. Pick them up as I leave the house."

"Mhmmn. On a night she would consider safe, Jan could take your office key to one of the discount stores. They stay open around the clock. It should be easy to detach the office key and take it to the place. She probably would not be out of the house more than an hour, and even if she kept it over a whole day you might not miss it. The office is usually open when you arrive."

Dick nodded. He glanced back over his shoulder at Gene's house. And sighed. "Why must we go into all this tonight?" he asked. "I'm tired. I got almost no sleep last night — family, coroner, autopsy — I've worked today, and done a few things for the family."

"I know, and I'd put this off if I thought it the thing to do. But I'll show you that it is important for us to get on it for tonight."

"I hope so," Dick grumbled.

"You're worried about Gene, and want to be with him. But let me show you this one thing, then I'll take over."

"Cops and robbers."

"That's right." He had, by then, driven out of the suburb into the city. The single houses drew closer to one another, apartments rose thickly, and showed their age. Tall business buildings appeared, and they, too, became dark with soot and stains of the years. The streets were dark with their looming bulk, and the sidewalks were busy with the people of the ghetto. Again there were apartments and everywhere the signs of poverty, or at least need. And some store windows were bright, others dark and unwashed. Finally at a corner, there was one, with a notably snow-white half curtain drawn across the window. And a name, a square cross — both gold-outlined on red.

HEALTH CENTER, the sign said.

And beside the door, in smaller letters, the hours and days that the health center would be open.

And, covering the whole front door was a sign:

OPEN SATURDAY, November 26.
10 A.M. to 4 P.M.

The next day.

Kenny drove slowly past. Dick stared at the store front.

"With our supplies," he said, unbelieving.

"Largely," said Kenny, increasing speed. "Jan gave them some furniture. Chairs, a table — everything a doctor's office and waiting room would need, more or less."

"The damned . . ." Dick began, and he added words slowly, bluntly. "What are we into, Kenny?"

"We go to court. And have the project stopped. No, not you, just now. I'll go tomorrow. Leslie and I got all the evidence. Next week you may have to appear at a court hearing."

Dick sighed. Next week, Lindsay's funeral would be done with. Gene must make plans — and, next week, Heidi Marie was starting for Europe. To spend Christmas, and then bring her father back with her. Reed had offered to go with her, but she was sure she could manage. Dick was sure she could, too. But she would be gone for six weeks, maybe two months, and — and —

Kenny was talking. ". . . felt we had to let you see this, and probably stop the guy before he actually went into practice. Besides, we were sure that all we have on Jan would give you a way out there . . ."

He stopped and looked at Dick, who was shaking his head. "I've had a way out for some time," he said. "A messy, dirty way —"

"This will be messy for Jackson. We'll get that injunction tomorrow, I am sure —" He pulled up beside Dick's car in the office building parking lot. Dick looked curiously at his keys as he took them out of his pocket.

"You'll have your hands full," he said. "But so will I tomorrow. And Sunday."

He was driving Heidi to the International Airport in St. Louis where she could get a direct flight to Frankfort. Her brother would meet her —

"But anything you need me for," he said alertly, "call on me. My position tonight and tomorrow is only that of chief worrier."

Kenny laughed. "That's better," he said approvingly. "I'm sorry we had to break it tonight. But this has gone on too long already."

"Yes, it has. We couldn't let that know-nothing begin to practice and charge people. I hope you get a good judge who will believe you."

"He already believes me."

"All right. Call me if you need me. Otherwise I'll be in the office Monday, or at all three hospitals. Whatever is needed. Jackson's going to be ugly."

"So is Jan."

Dick nodded. "Yes, she is. She will be."

He drove home and parked his car, then cut across to Gene's house. Marlene had put her husband to bed. "He talks too much," she whispered to Dick. "I suppose you know that Regina died this evening."

He turned sharply. "No!"

"It's a blessing. I supposed that was where you were."

"Oh, Lord!"

"Leona wants no funeral for her. But she will be buried beside her father."

"I'll go to the house."

"Yes, do that. But speak to Gene first."

"And you make me a milk shake or something nourishing."

"To last until tomorrow. That's going to be quite a day."

It was quite a day, beginning with Dick's going to Children's Hospital and as the doctor of record, signing the death certificate for Regina Tabler.

At eleven, he took Marlene and Gene to the funeral, and kept his hand on his brother's arm. "You're feeling my pulse," Gene whispered.

"Damned right I am."

"Don't swear in church."

Dick smiled weakly.

Only Lindsay's family went to the cemetery. Dick went home with Gene and Marlene, and at two he had a call from Dr. Harrington. Could Dick possibly come to Judge Severn's chambers? There was a charge Jackson was threatening to bring.

Dick said he would come. "What about the newspapers?"

"I can talk to them."

"I'll be there."

The session in the Judge's chambers was a rough one. Jan was present and ready to accuse Dick of being indifferent to the needs of the poor. Yes! She had helped Jackson get things together for the clinic!

Jackson was even more defiant. And offered the information that Dr. Foster did weird things like putting pictures of babies dead at birth into frames which were then set into a tombstone . . .

"Was that explained to the Judge?" asked Sister, when Dick came to tell her of the event.

"Later it was explained. Then, he said we should stick to the subject at hand. And we did. I established Jackson's medical status, and he was told to return everything he had stolen. Jan was to do what she could about the lease on the storefront."

"And she was upset."

"She was. I have several messes to clean up there. I only hope Jackson doesn't decide to be ugly to Leslie. I'm leaving town tomorrow."

She smiled at him. "Yes, I know," she said softly.

Everyone knew about his affairs. Which was all right. He didn't have much explaining to do.

The next day it was snowing. Hard. Marlene said they should not drive. The Interstate was already blocked at Columbia.

"We don't need to drive. We can fly across state. I'll call Heidi."

When he called the Crans house, Reed

told him to go to a certain address. Heidi was there, with a surprise.

"We were going to drive to St. Louis —"

"I know. Please do as she asks."

He would always do as Heidi asked. So he dressed for the trip, put his medical bag and a small carry-on with clothes enough should he decide to stay overnight, and, consulting his note, he drove to the address which Reed had given him. There had been something in the fellow's voice. Laughter? Excitement? Something was going on.

The address was that of a fine, old home. He parked, went up the steps, and found four doorbells and name cards beside the front door. An apartment house. One of the cards just read *Kreuger.* He touched the button, frowning. What was going on now? These days . . .

"Yes?" came a voice from the tube.

"Dr. Foster calling."

"Oh, Dick! Come in!"

He heard the lock click, he opened the door and entered a wide hall with oak paneling, oak doors, a stairway — and Heidi's pretty face popped out of the door to the left. She wore a blouse and skirt, and an apron! To travel? He went toward her. Ready to explain that they could fly to St. Louis.

"Come in, come in," she said.

"But, Heidi —"

She held out her hand. "It is all right," she assured him. So he crossed the hall and followed her through the tall door into a pleasant room. Bay windows curtained in crisp white, draperies which could be drawn. An Oriental rug, a fire on the hearth, a black cat stretching to sit up and look at him with slanted golden eyes. And seated in an armchair, a cane leaning against the arm of it, a white-haired gentleman who looked so much like Heidi —

She almost danced in her excitement. "Welcome to our home, Doctor!" she cried, her voice lilting with pleasure. "And may I present you to my father, Herr — No! *Professor* Kreuger, who has come himself to live in America!"

Dick went across to shake the old gentleman's hand. Like many paralytics, he felt obliged to explain his condition.

"Yes, I understand," said Dick, sitting on a small chair. "You can walk? Good! And talk?"

"Not — so — good," the Professor managed. "My right hand . . ."

"The two things go together," said the doctor. "Have you had therapy? Exercises? Good."

He glanced at Heidi. "How . . . ?"

"He called me three nights ago. The night Mr. Tabler died. Thanksgiving. A friend was coming to America. He would be pleased to escort my father. We found this apartment. Though the Crans's would have welcomed him. And now we have a home, and I am cooking dinner for you."

"And the cat?"

"Oh, I have had the cat at the Crans's. He is a Burmese."

"I should call my answering service," said Dick.

"You were giving me the long day."

"Yes, but I might be needed."

"There is a telephone in the kitchen," she agreed. "Please look at our comfortable apartment."

It was a comfortable one. It had belonged to the house owner, and was rented only to special people. Dick spent a pleasant day in it. The snow outside, the fire within, the black cat purring on his knee. He offered to get wine. He turned to Heidi's father. "Perhaps you think Americans cannot make wine. I can get whatever you would like."

"There is no need to go out," said Heidi. "I bought some Burgundy yesterday, and my dear father approved of it."

It was a pleasant day. To sit there and

watch Heidi move about. Cooking the meal, coming in to sit with them, serving — talking. Her father watched them both. And what he saw must have been the quiet, the love, the grace that there was between the big, blond man and his daughter.

Heidi talked of her studies, her work at the hospital. "Where this doctor is very important!" she said. "But I am no longer afraid of him, because he has become my friend."

Was she reassuring the invalid? That was the best way, thought Dick.

After the ones which had preceded it, this was a happy day, and he was content. It could not last. Here again was a situation where he must do something. He could not say to this old-world gentleman, not this one, "I am in love with your daughter. But I cannot ask you to allow me to marry her."

He must *do* something!

For now, he could only sigh. And he asked Heidi if she knew how to copy a key.

At first she laughed. "I don't think I understand you . . ." she said. *"Bitte?"*

Only occasionally did they have language difficulties. "I said . . ."

"You asked me if I could copy a key."

They spoke softly. The Herr Professor had dozed off. The fire whispered and the snow touched the windows with light fingers.

He laughed. "I asked you — Oh, it makes no difference."

The Professor stirred. "If I were your age, and able," he said, "I would go for a walk in this snow."

"The Doctor does not have boots," said Heidi.

"I do in the car," said Dick. "I keep them there, winter and summer."

"Then I shall put on mine, fetch yours, and we shall walk."

"And you can tell him that you do not know how to copy a key," said her father.

Heidi lifted her eyebrows, and went to change to slacks, knee-high boots, a heavy jacket, and a knitted cap. Dick gave her the keys of his car and she found the boots. He pulled his tweed hat down over his ears, turned up the collar of his overcoat, and they departed, laughing, slipping; they had promised Heidi's father to return in an hour. And they had a good walk in the little park across the street from the big house where the Kreugers lived. The street lights went on, and the snow stopped. The plows could be heard on the highway. Dick kissed Heidi's cold, pink cheek.

She laughed into his eyes. "No," she said,

"I do not know how to copy a key. Is it important? I suppose I could find out. Once I think I saw on TV that an impression was made on wax . . ."

He kissed her cheek again. "I like you, Heidi," he said warmly. "Let's go back."

They did go back, and Dick did not take off his wraps. He went directly to Professor Kreuger. "Someday," he said, "I shall ask to be allowed to marry your daughter."

The old gentleman smiled faintly. "When you are free, do ask me," he said quietly.

Dick went home then, stopping to check on Gene. He had already gone to bed. "Talked out," said Marlene. "You made a quick trip."

He told her what had happened, and she said that was good.

"Yes, it is good. But now I must do something about Jan."

"We've never been able to understand why you stayed with her for so long."

"My medicine was more important than anything else. She made me a comfortable home —"

"But now you want more."

"Now I mean to have more."

Marlene patted his shoulder. "For tonight, go work on your little furniture," she said. "You always find that quieting."

At midday dinner, Heidi had told her father about the miniatures which Dick made. They had talked of fine woods and veneers.

The whole day had made a bright spot in his life. On Monday, he could take up his work with calm and precision as was the custom with him.

The case of Regina Tabler was brought up in staff meeting at Children's. It was agreed that her death was unavoidable, and fortunate that it came when it did.

Dick went to the three hospitals, he kept his office hours, cared for old patients, and a few new ones. A man with psoriasis, a child with measles whose mother got a gentle lecture on immunization, and told not to take the boy through the waiting room again lest there be a pregnant woman out there. All the routine things, he did. He talked to Kenny about Jackson and what the court would do.

"And Leslie will have to identify all the stuff that belongs to us," said Kenny.

"Doesn't it all?"

"Jackson says not."

Dick's opinion of what Jackson said made everyone within hearing laugh.

It was a normal day; yesterday's beautiful snow was reduced to salt-blackened slush at the sides of the streets and roads. Besides Jackson, other things kept intruding. Dick thought about Gene and his problems. He must find an hour to go see Leona and talk to her about Lindsay and the little girl who had died. Lindsay had not had medical attention; the baby was an unfortunate situation from which she was released. She would feel guilty about both of them, but Dick could cut that guilt in half.

And of course he thought about Heidi. Little bits and pieces of the day before kept coming into his mind. He found himself to be eager about her, to see her, to hear her voice, to touch her. Yesterday she had revealed, and her father had discussed her feeling that she must not consider marriage; that it was her duty — and, she added — her pleasure, to care for her father. But she had come to America, and, her father said, of course she must hold herself ready to marry, to have children. Laughing, Dick said that he heartily agreed.

The Professor said, a twinkle in his very blue eyes, that it was nonsense for her to think she must stay with him every hour, every minute. She must continue her studies, she must on three days a week do the hospital work which she seemed to enjoy so much. And she must feel free to do any other things she would find beneficial or enjoyable.

Meanwhile he would do his own things. He would go to the University where he would have an office and a library to control. Young Mr. Crans had already secured someone to take him there each day, and home again. He did not want to feel that he must look out for Heidi. They had laughed happily about this speech which he made with some difficulty, and laughed again when he said it was harder to speak English than it was German.

Dick told of his small success in learning the scientific German that had been required when he studied medicine.

This led to Heidi's telling about the docent program and how skilled Dr. Foster was at guiding would-be doctors through the maze of medical procedure, ethics, and doing without sleep.

"You are speaking of Reed Crans," Dick pointed out. "I was not as good with some of the other students. Of course Alice Baus learned —"

But he had gone on to talk for fifteen minutes about the docent program, arguing its benefits and its failures.

He did not mention Jackson, but the man was in his mind. Thinking of him, Dick said thoughtfully that he may have been the wrong man to choose as a docent. Truesdell was, knew it, and quit. "I decided that I was bound to learn what I needed to know, and I stuck with it; maybe I'll do better another year."

"Do they have a different group of doctors each year?" Heidi asked.

"The matter is being discussed. Of course Truesdell will be replaced, and there are those who think that the students should benefit by experience gained, that we should not subject them to the same mistakes each year. So I am afraid we are stuck with the thing. Good or bad, the results seem to be the fault of the doctors."

It all made for a good day.

On Tuesday morning, he saw Heidi again. In her striped apron and white blouse, she was wheeling a cart full of toddlers down the hall to their play-therapy session. She greeted the big man in white as gaily as did the children. One little girl wanted to be kissed. Dr. Foster obliged, and turned to Heidi. "Can I kiss you, too?" he asked.

She laughed. "We'd both be fired."

"Well, that might be fun, and certainly a change." So he did kiss her. And nothing happened. Though they each knew that something had. Dick watched her and the cart turn in at swinging double doors. He went to the floor desk and read charts. "102" he wrote on the margin of the chart, and scrubbed it out. That was *his* pulse, not the child's.

From the chart desk he went to the doctors' lounge for coffee and to change back into street clothes. He wanted to hang around Children's all morning, just on the chance of seeing Heidi again. She made him feel so *good!*

"What are you grinning about?" asked Kenny Harrington, who was waiting for an appendix case, six years old, to recover from anesthesia.

Dick pulled off his white jumper, and unfastened the top button on his ducks. "I'm happy," he said. "I think I am going to be married."

"You've gone *loco*," said one of the other doctors. "You *are* married."

Dick stepped out of the white trousers. "Do you really think so?" he asked. "Believe me, sonny, sleeping on a couch, or even on a single bed alone in a room, is not being married. Not even a foam mattress makes it so."

"But you also have your good-looking girl friend."

Dick turned away from the locker, his face

puzzled. Had someone seen him kiss Heidi?

Kenny stood up. "Leslie is a well-kept secret around here," he said dryly.

"Oh!" said Dr. Foster. "I see. But what you wise guys don't know is that I haven't dated Leslie since I met this new girl. Now, with Leslie, it's strictly dictate, sign letters, and all such between me and the 'girl friend.' "

"Who's the new girl?" asked Kenny, going to the telephone to inquire about his patient. He gave his name. "Give me the status on the Winkler boy," he said. Then, "Thank you."

He returned to his chair, and asked Dick if he had heard the name right.

"Did you get your stats right?"

"Oh, yes, I did that. But this Swiss miss —"

"I plan to marry her. And she is not Swiss."

"But there will be a little talk about that, too, Doctor," said Dr. Harrington, whose beeper was sounding.

Dick laughed. "I'll guarantee that there will be," he said.

"But why not, pardner?" asked Kenny, lingering at the door. "Miss Kreuger is a swell girl. Pretty as a Christmas-tree angel, but she's been a volunteer here for two or three years, and only now you're . . ."

"She's been here about one year," said Dick, knotting his tie. He explained about her coming as an AFS student, her father's stroke, the kindness of the Crans family. "And now they've arranged for the father to come here. He has a job at the University, and Heidi —"

"I see," said Kenny. "But if she's all that good, why hasn't she married before now? Reed Crans is a very good catch."

"And he has another girl. Heidi — She's felt her obligation to go home and care for her father. I think that's a reason. Maybe she's only particular." He smiled smugly.

"You're serious, aren't you?" Kenny asked when they were out in the hall.

"I certainly am. And nineteen-years-old in love. I myself cannot imagine that she's been here for a year and I just found her. So it's all brand-new."

"He's happy about something," the floor nurse told Dr. Harrington as they both watched Dick stride down the hall.

"He deserves it," said Kenny. "I'm going up to Recovery."

"Yes, Doctor." The nurse watched him go, as she had watched Dr. Foster. Were both men forgetting, as they should not, that Foster's wife — a wasp of a woman — and his secretary, pleasant, voluptuous, generous, could both make trouble for the likable, and now happy, doctor?

Chapter 9

Lindsay Tabler had been dead for almost a week, his funeral was five days behind them, yet, Gene complained, Dick still watched him like a hawk.

"If someone," Dick retorted, "had been watching Lindsay as closely, he would still be alive, and I wouldn't have to make like a hawk."

"I can't understand his not having a doctor," said Gene. "We slipped up there. I am ordering everyone in the business to have a physical checkup."

"Where?"

"The employees are voting. We can select a plant doctor, or have a list of approved ones."

Marlene smiled at Dick. "I'll bet you get caught either way," she said.

"I'll bet I do, too. Well, I'd better get home for supper. I haven't been there too regularly lately."

"Has Jan noticed?"

Dick shook a reproving finger at her. "She mentioned it this morning." He had thought she was going to speak a piece about Jackson. This was inevitable, but must be got through. He had not seen the tall, handsome fellow anywhere since the shutting down of his "clinic." That may have made the papers, but Lindsay's death and his Sunday with the Kreugers, catching up on his office work, his concern for Gene and his business problems —

Good Lord, he had had little time to notice Jan's presence or absence. He was surprised to find breakfast prepared for him that morning, and to have her come in from the yard to ask him to try to make it home for dinner.

She did not have to explain that she had some talking to do.

He nodded, and said that he would try. Which was what he always said. No, he added, that morning, he did not have any meeting scheduled.

This satisfied her, and she went back to whatever it was she had been doing outside. Washing her car, he found, when he finished his breakfast and went out. Before this he had asked her why she didn't have it done.

"I like to clean things," she explained.

So that morning he only glanced at her. Denim slacks, a striped blouse hanging out below an old sweater, and her dark hair straggling across her forehead. As always.

He backed his own car out, lifted his hand in farewell, and drove away. He had a full schedule, including Mrs. Parks, for the day.

But he was home by six o'clock, looking as well pressed and neat as when he had left that morning. "Do I have time for a shower?" he asked. His rose bed needed attention, and if dinner didn't last too long . . . It wouldn't. But all signs said that Jan had something to talk about. Well, so did he.

Refreshed by the warm shower and loose clothing, a corduroy jacket and slacks, with a turtleneck pullover, he came down and enjoyed the pot roast which Jan had prepared; there were dumplings, and a good fruit salad for dessert. He asked her if she had seen Gene or Marlene during the day.

"Marlene drove Gene somewhere. To the plant, I suppose. What's going to happen there, now?"

"Something will be arranged. Gene has returned to being president instead of chairman of the board."

"And all that stock he gave Lindsay is now Leona's."

"I believe the will read that she was his sole heir."

"Did he have a controlling interest?"

"No But if other stockholders complied,

it would amount to that."

"What if Leona marries again?"

"There's that chance. She's a young woman, and attractive."

"Well, young at least."

It was typically a Jan remark and Dick had learned to ignore them, not rise to their bait.

"Is there some way for Gene to get that stock back?"

"Well, I suppose he could buy it. Leona may want him to. I really do not know. I avoid bringing up issues with Gene. He thinks up enough for himself."

"Could Gene live and take care of the business himself?"

Suddenly, Dick knew that he was tired, and that he had many things on his mind. "Maybe," he said shortly. "I certainly hope he will live." He rose to answer the telephone.

He had been hoping that he might stop to see Gene, and then go to Heidi for an hour. That he desperately wanted to do!

But the phone call —

When he came back to the dining room, Jan was clearing the table. "I thought you said . . ."

"I did say. I wanted to talk to you. But they've called a meeting on the docent program. Whether they vote to continue it, or stop it, my immediate future is involved."

"Oh, go on," she said, not caring for his explanation.

He looked at his watch. The roses would be hilled another day, or night, he would look in on Gene, and go downtown — and he was, as he said, truly sorry.

"You can reach me through the answering service," he told Jan as he left the house.

She did not answer.

Perhaps the meeting would not take long, but it did. Too long for him to stop at Heidi's. A doctor should be as celibate as a priest, Dick told himself. There were so many demands made upon him. But of course he had expected this meeting. The docent program was important. There were several questions to answer. Was it to resume during the spring term of pre-medical school? Should other doctors take over? Maybe first year of medical would be better than the last year of pre-med.

"And I'd get Jackson and the other creeps again," Dick murmured to Kenny.

Kenny was being selected to take Truesdell's place. Which was not, Dick pointed out, a really good choice. Both of them primary doctors, sharing the same offices.

Utley suggested that Dick give them an

idea of the strength and the weaknesses of the program.

"You know them."

"But I don't have your organized mind. So let's list them off."

"I'll try. There are more weaknesses than strengths. It all depends on the students we get. I've had a couple of really good candidates. But the big thing with me is that some student, or students, get the idea that three months with the docent teaches them all they need to know to be a doctor."

There was discussion about this, and Dick's thoughts wandered for a few minutes to the miniature mountain cabin he planned to make for Heidi. A log cabin, one room and a loft; at one end of the dirt-floored main room a four-poster oak bed, a stone fireplace at the other. Red and white checked curtains, a straw pallet in the loft. A rocking chair. Could he do it by Christmas? He would certainly try. He —

"Dick, do you think first year of medical school would be better than senior premed?" The direct question brought him back into focus.

"I think a more sophisticated docent program could be devised for medical school. The one we have had was to help students decide if they actually wanted to study medicine."

"But you don't think we should abandon the whole project?"

"My bones think I should. It takes a lot of time. But if it does any good, we should continue, and improve on what we have been doing. Now we are talking, I hope, about physicians, not specialists. We are talking about a way of life which a young man or woman may or may not want to pursue.

"There's another thing. In organizing our medical school it was stated that our purpose was to turn out clinicians, rather than do research or teach research. That can come later. So the docents should be models of such clinicians. Truesdell knew that. I suspect Dr. Utley knows it." He glanced across at his friend, who nodded.

"Perhaps in the last year of medical school we could establish some sort of docent program to determine specialties," he said.

Dick nodded. "My thought is that community physicians as well as the staff members of our medical school and the participating departments of the university should make decisions for the school through an elected council. Working committees will handle details. The deanship should be occupied by a tenured faculty member for only a certain period of time, say seven years, with an additional term possible. As long as the term is temporary it will present a challenge.

"But we should encourage students to become family physicians. It is obvious, at least to me, that the American public needs care from doctors who can know all aspects of the patients. Family practice supplies that kind of care."

"What," asked Dr. Utley, "about the claim that family practice is shrinking?"

"You're right," said Dick quickly, and Kenny looked up alertly. "If it is shrinking, it would do no good to offer programs geared to it. But I am proceeding on the premise I make that it is not falling off, and I am working toward helping the patients of it. If you can find a chair, come in and watch the parade through my waiting room someday, any day, and listen in this evening when Kenny or I speak to the answering service."

"Will you take charge of the docent program, Dr. Foster?" asked the Director respectfully.

"No, sir, I won't. I am entirely too busy. And right now it looks as if I were going to be busier."

He talked to Kenny, and he talked to Gene, and by the next Sunday he was ready, he said, to ask Jan for a divorce.

"She'll ask for a tremendous alimony," both men assured him.

Dick waited. He was ready for her demands.

"If you file, and can prove her denial of your marital rights —" Gene persisted.

Dick could. Jan had done some bragging about her way with her man; the docent students who had lived in the house knew that she locked her bedroom door.

"Well, at least," said Kenny in exasperation, "talk to Jim Wakefield."

Wakefield was their attorney, and had done a fine job for them at various times, especially about Jackson's pilferings. He had been able to put the fear of God into that young buckaroo.

"I plan to consult Jim," Dick said now.

It was Kenneth who suggested that Leslie might make trouble.

"She might," Dick agreed. "Though I've done well by her. But she wants to go to Miami with me next week. When I tell her she can't, and why, I'll handle the row she'll make."

Kenny put both hands over his ears.

"I've made it clear," said Dick, "from the first, that marriage would never be in the picture for me."

"Yes. Her sort don't want the risk of marriage. But they like to be sure of their place."

"She was sure. And she can hold her job here, if she wants. I hope she does, but the travel is out."

Kenny shrugged and started to walk away. Then he came back. "What about your girl?" he asked.

"Heidi?" Dick's face lit up like a full moon. "Oh, she says she loves me, and with her —"

"You two didn't lose any time."

"Neither of us had any time to waste."

"Will she stand for the dust Jan and Leslie can kick up?"

"I hope there won't be a lot of dust. But, yes, Heidi will take it. She'll do better than stand for it; she'll fight for it. For me. She is convinced that we can marry, take care of her father, and have a home. She says that is what she wants, and she knows she cannot have it unless we do marry."

The two men laughed. "Good girl!" said Kenny, once more starting to leave.

"Isn't she!" said Dick heartily. "And since she is setting the rules —"

"The woman always does. Doesn't she?"

Dick shrugged. "It's their strength. As for me, I like it. This time I will."

Chapter 10

There was to be a meeting about Gene's business, and the night before it was to take place Marlene asked Dick for his help. Gene had agreed to go to bed early, and Marlene had asked Dick to come over to the house. "Quietly," she said.

"Is something wrong?" Dick had been dreading a letdown for Gene ever since Lindsay's death. Up to now he had held up well, but reactions were common, and his would be a serious development.

"No," said Marlene. "He said he wanted to get his beauty sleep before the meeting tomorrow."

Dick laughed and said he would come over. Yes, quietly.

Marlene was waiting at the door. "I don't want Gene to hear us."

"Good heavens, girl!" He dropped his coat on a chair.

There was a fire on the living-room hearth, and Marlene offered him coffee. A drink of some sort?

He patted the cushion of the couch. "You

just sit down and tell me what's on your mind," he said. "I can see you are flustered over something."

"I am," she agreed. She drew a thin gray shawl about her shoulders. "I chill in this kind of weather," she explained.

Dick waited.

"The thing I'm flustered about," she said then, "is Leona."

Lindsay's wife. Marlene had never really liked the younger woman, who was competent, and had made a good home for her husband and child. She had borne poor little Regina, but certainly that was no fault of hers. Those things happened.

"She sees herself sitting in Lindsay's chair," Marlene was saying. "She wants to be manager of the company."

Dick considered this. "In time," he agreed, "perhaps she could do it. But she evidently knows that she has much to learn."

"She should know it, but now she owns all that stock —"

Yes, she did.

"Gene can't help it," said Gene's wife tensely, "and he must not try!"

"I don't think he plans to, Marlene."

"I have stock, too. In my name!"

"Yes, I know you do. You are a rich woman."

"I could learn to manage the business. If Leona can, I can."

Dick was troubled. He did not want a family quarrel among the women. "Leona may want to learn to do it, dear. Are you sure that you do? What happens to Gene while you are working in the offices, going off to sales meetings?"

"Leona has a child."

"And you don't like her. Leona, I mean."

"No," said Marlene, "I don't."

"This worries Gene."

Marlene looked at him, puzzled. "Oh, dear . . ." she said uncertainly. "What would you do, Dick? In my place?"

He picked up a round orange pillow and bounced it between his hands. "I'd do," he said slowly, "the job I am good at."

Marlene thought that over. "If Leona would try it," she said, "she might find she couldn't do it."

"That could happen."

"And she might even get married again, to some man who —"

Dick put the cushion back into its place. "Yes," he said, "that could happen also. I almost hope it won't. She's been married to Lindsay for seven or eight years; it would be difficult to settle for a poorer image. Of course the man need not be one."

"He would be, in her eyes. I know how I'd feel after being Gene's wife. But what about you and Jan, dear? Isn't there some way . . . ?"

"Not Leona, dear matchmaker. Anyway, now I have Heidi."

"Tell me about her." Marlene settled into the couch corner. "Reed says she's a doll, whatever that means."

"It means Heidi. And she is a doll. I knew it the minute I saw her." So he talked for ten minutes about Heidi, his face glowing. Marlene watched him, hopeful for him.

"If Jan won't give you a divorce . . ."

"She'll give me one now," said Dick confidently. "I'm all set to tell her so."

Marlene stood up. "Then you get along home. But don't tire yourself out. I think Gene wants you at the meeting tomorrow."

"He mentioned it, and I suppose my three shares of stock qualifies me. But something could come up, Marlene. And I promise you, I won't vote to have you as president or manager or whatever job it was Lindsay held."

She laughed. "I didn't bring you over here to get your vote. But I would feel better if you were there. Gene gets excited, but not as excited when you're watching him."

"I'll do my darnedest to be there. It's on

my schedule. What about Jan?"

"She doesn't own any stock."

"And I hope she doesn't know there is to be a meeting. I don't want her there."

"Have you talked to her about a divorce? Does she know about Heidi?"

"I suppose so. She knows almost everything. I started to talk to her. I have a proposition to put to her which she just may accept."

"Don't give her your house."

"I won't and she wouldn't take it. But we'll see. It would have been handled by now, but Lindsay's death came on us like a blow from a sledgehammer. I think Jan could be into some hot water, if I need to bring pressure. What's more, I think she knows it. But let's forget it for tonight. And I hope we get through the meeting with Gene as calm and satisfied as he can be."

He went home and to bed without mentioning the meeting for the next day. Jan most certainly would insist on attending, and her presence alone would upset Gene. And Marlene.

The stockholders' meeting was held, as scheduled, the next morning. Not a very large meeting; Dick came in as it was about to begin, and he saw the look of relief on his brother's face, wiping the tenseness away. These were the stockholders, and as chairman of the board, Gene was to preside. He begged permission to turn this task over to the man who had been Lindsay's assistant. He glanced at Dick, who nodded in approval.

His brother gave him a second glance. Dick was looking well this morning in a tweed suit, blue shirt, and tie. Come to think of it, he had been looking well for some time now. Even in spite of Lindsay's death.

Dick moved his chair to a position at Gene's shoulder. "Pay attention," he said softly. He glanced about the room. Tension was visible throughout. The selection of a new manager, or president, was important. It might be that the family would want to dissolve the business. Yes, there was tension.

As soon as the minutes of the last meeting were brought up, a motion was made and a vote taken to dispense their reading. Copies had been sent to all owners. As soon as a formal resolution was read concerning the death of Lindsay Tabler, Lindsay's wife was on her feet, asking for the floor. Dick would not look at Marlene. He knew what she was expecting. Gene sat quiet.

Leona was a tall woman, too slender

lately, her face too drawn with the griefs of the past weeks. She had dark hair, shoulder length, and she brushed it back, to fall in the frame for her face, cupping under her chin. That day she wore a dark dress, simple to plainness, and no jewelry except her wedding ring, which she turned with the fingers of her right hand as she spoke.

"Be better if she'd prettied up," murmured Gene.

"Listen," Dick advised him.

Leona was asking to be allowed to speak first. Her voice shook with nervousness. Her gaze flicked from one face to the other. Dick felt sorry for her. "I think," she said. "I think I can get this discussion on the right path. I don't know the etiquette or the procedure, as you probably already know . . ." She broke off and was silent for a second, twisting her ring. Then she looked up. "The thing I want to do," she said, "is to return the stock in this company, the stock which Gene gave to Lindsay . . ." Whatever else she may have said was lost in a rumble of surprise and protest.

Dick watched the young woman, feeling himself relax. Marlene had been wrong, Jan had been wrong. Leona had not thought . . .

He looked at his brother, who was faintly smiling. He was a good judge of people. And Marlene was trying to get on her feet. She dropped her purse, she dropped her pencil and little notebook she had been holding.

Dick bent over to retrieve her belongings. "Say your piece," he said over his shoulder.

"All right, I will," said his sister-in-law. "I don't think it would be right for Leona to give that stock back. Or, at least, she could sell it; the company should buy it. Shouldn't they, Gene?"

He was laughing. Dick handed her the pencil she had dropped and which she now tucked into the knot of gray curls atop her head. She almost always kept a pencil there. "I didn't say it right, did I?" she asked.

"You did fine, sweetheart," said Gene. "Sit down now, and quit dropping things. Leona wants to talk."

The tension had lightened visibly. There were smiles on several faces. Leona saw this, or sensed it. She rested her hands on the back of a chair. "Thank you, Marlene," she said. "But you know I shall have to go to work somewhere. And, here and now, I am going to ask if I could have a job with the company, with the hope of sometime moving to a desk in Lindsay's office, his department, to learn the work done there. I would work very hard. And I already know quite a lot. Really, I do. Because Lindsay would talk to me. He'd tell me things that had happened, talk over little problems he had. I didn't go to the office much, but I got to know the people he worked with from his talk about them. All the people, his secretary, the receptionist, the men on what he called 'the line.' He meant, I think, those who moved the machinery around. Brought it in, set it in display order, delivered it. He would draw charts and discuss where items would show best. I wasn't any help, but he could trust me, and talk out his problems. If some worker had problems, he would tell me, and we would try to solve the matter. So — well, I would like a job. Receptionist, typist. I can make out sales slips, can bill —"

Her voice trailed away, and she sat down. "So now you know what I am asking you to decide," she said.

There was a spatter of applause, and Gene reached over to hug her shoulders. "Good girl," he said. "Good girl."

Marlene whispered to Dick. "Should I apologize?"

"What for? You didn't say anything except to me. And you know what a bottomless well a doctor can be."

Within a half hour, things were settled. Leona would have a job, at a salary, and she was to keep the stock, offering the company the right to purchase on demand.

The meeting dispersed, Gene going off with Dick. Marlene had the car, but Gene had things to attend to. And speaking in unison, or just about, the two men said to each other that they must acknowledge that Leona had always been behind Lindsay's success.

"I admire her immensely," said Gene. "But —"

"Marlene admires her too," Dick assured him. "She may have been a little jealous —"

"No reason."

"A woman doesn't always need a reason. I am wondering if, under similar circumstances, Jan would act as well."

Gene caught at his arm. "Hey!" he cried. "You're not —"

Dick shook him off. "Oh, no. But changes are coming, big brother. And I was wondering how the women in my life would take them. Leona, this morning, went far to restore my faith in women's unselfishness. Have I told you about Heidi?"

"Not enough. I want to meet her, to know her."

"You will, you shall."

"If you want her . . ."

"I mean to have her."

"Janice will be your big hurdle."

"Oh, yes. But now I can make it, and will."

"Will you eat lunch with me?"

"No. I am going straight home to tell Janice what is going to happen."

"Tell her what happened this morning."

"I shall, but the main thing —"

Gene nodded, and watched Dick walk down the corridor. "I wish I were a praying man," he said, half aloud. "Or maybe I wish there were no need for prayer. Maybe between now and afternoon office hours . . ."

There was time. As Dick drove into their property, he slowed to admire the two houses which the Fosters had built. Gene's red brick, Dick's white-painted one — the hill rising behind them, some of the trees still green. In summer they made a fine backdrop. But today, above their tops, brilliant in the sunlight against the blue sky, there was a froth of clouds. "Beautiful," he said softly, and drove on to the garage.

He found Jan at the house door, waiting for him.

"It's early for lunch," Dick said mildly. "I just had things to tell you."

"And I have things to tell you," she said. "An ultimatum, in fact."

Dick almost laughed. Which certainly would not have helped any, but he had thought he was the one to bring ultimatums.

They sat at the kitchen table, because they had entered the house through the kitchen.

Jan began by offering to fix lunch.

"Too early," said Dick. "The meeting wasn't very long."

"Did it go all right?"

"Of course. Gene has a bad heart, but his mind is as good as it ever was. Let's hear about your ultimatum, then —"

Jan was ready, even anxious. "I suppose," she said, "I should begin by saying that I want you to move to a country practice."

"We've been all over that."

"Yes, we have. This time we'll settle it."

Dick reached for a lemon from the green bowl of fruit which centered the table. He rubbed its pungent rind with the tips of his sensitive fingers and hoped Jan would be quick, perhaps he could find Heidi and — His head went up. "What did you say?" he asked.

Jan nodded. "You never did listen to me. I said that if you were continuing your opposition to the country practice, I would get — file for — a divorce."

She waited for him to register what she had said. He looked at her warily. "What would that divorce cost me?" he asked. After all the years, it was a little strange to find himself on this side of the fence.

"You know the small farm, and the doctor's practice I've been hoping you would buy."

"I'm not moving, Jan."

"I don't want you to move. But I do want that property. I can make a living on the farm —"

"And the doctor's practice?"

"I have a man in mind."

He stared at her. "If you mean Jackson —"

"I do mean him. You have already approved his entrance to medical school."

"He couldn't be ready for five or six years, and you can't trust him. You know you can't."

"I know you have disliked him because he is black —"

"He has proven that he is untrustworthy. You'll be lucky if he doesn't involve you in that mess over the clinic he wanted to set up. But the trouble with Jackson, Jan, is not that he is black. He's smart; he could be as good a doctor as he thinks he already is. But the man does not want to play ball according to the rules of the game. To study, to learn, to begin small and grow —"

Jan sat leaning back in her chair, a faint smile on her lips. "Don't worry about my being involved in any legal suit," she said. "As his wife, I could not testify."

Dick was on his feet. "You wouldn't!" he cried.

"Oh, yes. And I'll see to it that he plays your game of baseball according to the rules. We'll have the farm, the house — he'll go to school, and then practice —"

"That's the way you think it will be?" asked Dick. He was feeling faint — well, dazed. After all these years —

"That's the way it will be," said Jan. "Jackson and I have it all planned. He already has a job in a pharmacy. I'll make the farm pay. I've given up on you —"

And together she and Dick could go to the court and have their marriage dissolved. Dick resisted his impulse to take out his handkerchief and mop his face. He must not jump up and down, he must not show his relief.

"If that really is what you want, Jan —"

She smiled. "It's been a long time since I've had what I wanted. Now it is time that I should."

Dick sat down again. "All right. You can talk to my attorney . . ."

"*Your* attorney? Not on your life! He's your friend."

"And he's a good lawyer. He'll take care of you. If I need someone, I'll get someone. I won't fight you, Jan. I stand ready to give you the farm you want."

She seemed puzzled. "But what about *you?*" she asked. "I've taken care of you for so long —"

Dick considered this. "Yes, I suppose you have," he said. She had bought his socks, cleaned his house. "But I'll get along," he said. It would seem that she did not know about Heidi, and he had thought —

Well — He listened to what she was saying. "You'll probably work too hard," she said, "and help Gene worry about his affairs."

"I probably shall," he agreed. "But I hope you will be happy in the new life you'll have. And find some man that you like better than you do me."

"I told you —"

But Jackson would never marry her. He was too smart. He would use her, and move on —

Did Dick owe Jan anything? He hoped not.

"You'll marry again," she said. "You're used to it."

Used to having a housekeeper, yes. He was. "Who knows?" he asked. "Until this last half hour I thought I was married."

Jan had turned away. "I suppose the deed to the farm and all would come with the divorce?"

"It will."

He put the lemon back in the bowl, and saw Jan's hand turn it to what she considered the proper position. He was going upstairs to pack a small bag. He would stay at the motel behind his office. He would now go straight to Heidi and tell her. He left the house, whistling softly. Not knowing that he did it. Jan was probably watching, listening. But he could not guess what she was thinking. Perhaps that they had wasted ten years. They had not. She had learned more than she realized, and Dick had been waiting for Heidi.

He found her and her father eating lunch, and he was welcomed with surprise. Would he join them? It was only soup and hot bread —

He set a chair up to the table, sat down, tasted the thick soup, then swiftly told what had happened. He turned to Professor Kreuger. "Now, sir, I may ask you for your daughter's hand."

The old gentleman struggled to bring forth the proper words. "I give it — gladly," he said. "You are a good man."

Dick caught at Heidi's hand. Her eyes were shining. He smoothed her thick hair. "I have to go to the office now," he said. "But at four, I'll pick you up. We'll take an hour —" He glanced at her father, who nodded.

"I have work to do until six," he said.

"Good! Is the University treating you well?"

"Very well," Heidi said for him. "They

fetch him, they bring him home. He has a good secretary, and two student helpers. He enjoys it."

Dick finished his soup, kissed Heidi and said he would be back at four.

"I can come to the office."

"I'd rather do it this way." He still had Kenny and Leslie — and Sister Alphonsus to tell. And a list of patients to care for. Prostates and vaginitis, chicken pox and an unexpected pregnancy. And Mrs. Parks, no doubt, with her cancer.

But at fifteen minutes after four he was back; leaving the lamps lighted for her father's return, they started out, darkness descending quickly upon the winter's day.

"Where are we going?" Heidi asked. He liked the faint perfume of aromatic herbs which she carried, in her thick hair, on her smooth cheek, in her clothing. Today she wore the blue reefer jacket over a turtleneck sweater and plaid skirt.

"I'll show you," said Dick. "And explain why we are going there." And again he told her of Jan's ultimatum.

"It seemed so strange, after all the times I have asked her for a divorce. She evidently had no idea that I had found you. I knew what I was waiting for, I knew what I had found — but Jan, the all-knowing, did not know that. I've never tried to hide you. I mean —"

Her fingers lightly touched his gloved hand on the car wheel. "I know what you mean," she said softly. "It has shone in your face since that first day in the parking lot when I had the flat tire."

"Everyone else has known." He was silent as he drove steadily along the two-lane road into the hills. "I guess the truth is," he said, "that there has been no communication between Janice and me. We talked — but there was no communication. Not even from the first. She thought sex meant marriage, but she had no taste for it. I was absorbed in getting my M.D. Basically, it was never a marriage, or if one, it was a bad one. My friends told me not to stay with it. Now I am glad that I did." His eyes slid, smiling to her.

"This Jackson you talk about. Reed Crans used to speak of him, also, but not very favorably. He did say he was handsome."

"He was. He is."

"Will Janice really marry him?"

Dick laughed, warmly, in his throat. "She would, I think, but Jackson is not going to marry her. He'll let her support him as long as he can, then walk out. He's a rascal."

Heidi repeated the word, translating it, repeating it. "Poor Janice," she said finally.

"Don't pity her!" said Dick sharply. He sounded angry, and Heidi protested.

"I'm not really angry," he said. "But I do believe I finally understand Janice, and —"

"You regret the lost years."

He slowed the car, turned to look at her. "I was just waiting for you to show up," he said. "I know that now."

"I have known you for over a year," said Heidi serenely.

"How's that?" Dick asked. "A year?"

"I have seen you in the hospital, the big blond man whom everyone liked. I too thought you very handsome. And Reed, at the Crans home, talks about you all the time. He said you raised roses, and made small furniture, mostly at night."

"And doctored — also at night."

"Yes, he said that you did, that you were kind and thoughtful. Oh, yes, I have known you."

"And you waited."

"Yes, I did. Where is it we go tonight?"

"You've been there before. I have a dear friend who lives up on that hill. We will go to see him sometime soon."

"Yes. I shall get to know all your friends and your family."

"You don't already know them, through Crans?"

"Oh, yes, I have met your brother and his wife. I hope they will like me, and your friends as well."

"How could they help it? And if you are good to me, as you will be, you will understand also that I can be somewhat sad about what is happening to Janice."

"Somewhat?" she repeated. "A little?"

"Yes. But she will have her confounded farm, and I'll have you, and our children."

He turned the car off the road, stopped and went to help Heidi to get out of it. She looked around in wonder. The woods, the matted grass and weeds. "The cemetery again?" she asked.

"Yes." He took a small package from his coat pocket, and unwrapped it.

"The baby?" she asked.

"Yes. The original one. It was loose in the stone. I put in a replica while I — This is the one of the baby, born a hundred years ago. Born dead, probably, or perhaps died after a few weeks. The family put a photograph into this small tombstone. I built the frame up a little, and I thought that this evening was the time to put the original back where it belongs."

He went to the trunk of his car, and took out a small kit. There were tools, and cement. With a flashlight, he guided Heidi's feet in among the graves. He knelt and placed the glassed oval into the hole of the tombstone. "The baby belongs here," he said.

"Did someone try to dig the picture out?" asked Heidi, watching him work.

He did not lift his head. "I don't know that anyone did," he said quietly.

She sighed softly. "Then we have nothing to worry about."

Dick smiled at her, and smoothed his flattened hand down over the oval image which he had inserted, pressing it firmly into place. "This baby," he repeated, "belongs here. Its whole future belongs here. You know? I've become superstitious about this child. I want to work for its continued future. I have learned that a good future will come if we are patient, and do things right."

"And you will teach that to others," said Heidi, gazing at the oval-framed child. "Robin Hood," she said softly.

"Yes!" said Dick. "And I'll be a *geud* man too. Now that I shall have my future." He glanced up at her. "Won't I?"

He worked a little more with his chisel, his cement mix, his trowel. The future. Janice never knew that there was one. Leslie had never wanted one. But it was a lesson, indeed, that Dick knew and Heidi knew. He again pressed the picture back firmly into the stone. And Heidi watched him. She gave him a tissue and he wiped the glass — tenderly. "Now," he said, "we will leave the past where it belongs, knowing that we have our future."

"Wait," said Heidi. She knelt on the hard ground and murmured a few words. "It is a little German prayer," she said, rising. "I will teach it to you. I will teach you to understand German."

"Good luck!" said Dick, laughing. "It was the one subject I nearly flunked in college. But I think I could quote some English before our little monument. You know who Shelley the poet was?"

"Of course."

"Of course! Well, then — Let me remember. Here goes:

> '. . . those passions read
> Which yet survive,
> stamped on these lifeless things.' "

He touched the bit of curved glass, brushed his fingers across the old, old stone, took Heidi's hand, and they went back to the car, walking closely, warmly together.

We hope you have enjoyed this Large Print book. Other Thorndike Press or Chivers Press Large Print books are available at your library or directly from the publishers.

For more information about current and upcoming titles, please call or write, without obligation, to:

Thorndike Press
P.O. Box 159
Thorndike, Maine 04986 USA
Tel. (800) 257-5157

OR

Chivers Press Limited
Windsor Bridge Road
Bath BA2 3AX
England
Tel. (0225) 335336

All our Large Print titles are designed for easy reading, and all our books are made to last.